DEATH OF A SIREN

WILLIAM S. SCHAILL

DEATH
OF A
SIREN

A NOVEL

ACADEMY
CHICAGO

Copyright © 2016 by William S. Schaill, Trustee
All rights reserved
First edition
Published by Academy Chicago Publishers
An imprint of Chicago Review Press Incorporated
814 North Franklin Street
Chicago, Illinois 60610

ISBN 978-1-61373-426-1

Library of Congress Cataloging-in-Publication Data

Schaill, William S., 1944–
    Death of a siren / William S. Schaill. — First edition.
        pages ; cm.
    ISBN 978-1-61373-426-1 (softcover)
    I. Title.
    PS3569.C4725D43 2016
    813'.54—dc23
                                        2015033049

Cover design: Joan Sommers Design
Cover images: Photo montage by TJ Romero. Chart of the Galapagos
Islands 1798, Library of Congress. Island and woman photographs,
iStockphoto.
Interior design: PerfecType, Nashville, TN
Interior layout: Nord Compo

Printed in the United States of America
5 4 3 2 1

DEATH OF A SIREN

1

I wrapped the remains of my tattered canvas boat shoes around my feet and looked up at the strange building that was staring down at me. I then choked down the last of my foul water, which did little to quench my thirst, and manhandled the dinghy over the side of the boat. I hadn't seen any signs of life near the stone building, which I was already thinking of as "the castle," but there had to be some. Oddities like that don't just grow out of the ground on their own. Not even on an island so distant, ephemeral, and otherworldly that many doubted it ever existed, even 150 years after its discovery.

I rowed across the cove to the beach directly below the castle and sprang out into the shallow water. After hauling the dinghy up onto the stony beach, I paused again to catch my breath. From where I stood the building seemed shrouded in shadows. Whether this was due to the light or the angle from which I was viewing it or the color of the stones used to construct it I don't know. In fact, I didn't really care, since my mind was fixed at the moment on water. Cool, clear, fresh water. I sprinted up a path that led inland, the thin rubber soles of my shoes immediately proving no defense against the stony ground.

The ground leveled off fifty yards up the path. On either side I was surrounded by a small but prospering vegetable garden filled with tomatoes, spinach or some other green, and several kinds of beans. It was, I thought, a near miracle considering the dry, thin, sandy soil from which the plants were emerging. A miracle and the result of great labor. Twenty yards later I passed through a low hedge of cactus into a sort of formal garden. Various types of cactus and agave had been laid out in a pattern with paths running between the beds. Odd, I thought, but appropriate considering the soil. I continued through the prickly desert garden and found myself standing on a patio paved in what seemed an arbitrary pattern with the same tan, brown, and black volcanic rocks used in the rest of the construction. "Hello?" I shouted. "Is anybody here?"

There was no reply except the gentle flapping of what looked like a white curtain in one of the windows and the chirpy screeches of the little gray-brown finches that watched me from the surrounding dry brush.

The castle was considerably larger than I'd realized before. Another wing of rough, mottled stone stretched inland, away from the cove. On closer examination I could see there was no glass in the windows; the openings were protected only by crude wooden shutters. Directly ahead of me was a large opening in the stone wall, flanked by heavy doors of weathered wood planks. Inside, all I could see was darkness. It was like looking into the mouth of a deep cave that somehow absorbed the sunlight.

After almost three continuous months at sea, I was out of shape, sweating and puffing from the hike up from the beach. I paused to catch my breath. I watched as a little lizard chased an even smaller one up the stone wall. The lizards paused, the pursuer's throat puffing in and out like a kid's brightly colored balloon, shimmering slightly as it did. And then the chase was on again.

Time was passing, and my mouth felt as if it were filled with sand. Bold action was called for. "Hello?" I shouted again, then marched across the patio and through the double doors into a sort of great hall. On my second step I tripped over her.

As my eyes adjusted to the relative darkness I was able to clearly see a woman's body lying on the floor in front of a large, formal sofa. She was dressed in twill riding trousers and a khaki shirt, and she was drenched in blood. Blood that was no longer a lively, gem-like red but more of a restrained, dirt brown. She was lying on the brown-stained floor on her left side and bent slightly at the waist, as if she'd crumpled as she fell. Then I realized a hatchet was sticking out of the right side of her head and a riding crop was still clenched in her left hand.

I've dealt with more than my share of mangled, bloody bodies, bodies crushed by trucks or repeatedly shot or sliced to ribbons or drowned in their own bloody, diseased vomit, so I wasn't totally shocked. All the same, I was upset. I don't like seeing people die, and I don't want to die myself. Whenever I look at a dead body I always feel a little sad, even when I suspect the deceased deserved to die. More to the point, there was one dead body I would never get out of my mind—the body of the guy I killed. He deserved it, that's one thing I'm very sure of. Whether or not he should have died, however, is of only secondary importance. The important thing is that his death was the cause of my many current problems.

My thirst momentarily forgotten, I leaned over what was left of the woman and took a closer look. She had chestnut hair and was far from old. Early middle age at most—about my age. If she were still alive she'd have been very attractive, although it was hard to be sure with all the blood on her face and head. When she was younger she probably had been beautiful.

Sitting off to one side was a heavy polished mahogany coffee table with four or five empty beer bottles on it, along with maybe half a dozen rocks of various colors. All had a vaguely metallic, oily cast. Decorations of some sort, I assumed. Somebody, maybe the dead woman, was a rock collector.

The woman seemed to me totally out of place, as did the polished, carefully crafted furniture, so foreign to the rustic, crude architecture of the building. Who was she? What was she doing here? Where had she and the furniture come from? Why was she dead?

"Ilse!"

I turned to find a man dressed in long trousers and an undershirt standing behind me, staring at the corpse. He was tall and stringy with close-cut gray hair and an almost skeletal face. On that face was the strangest look I've seen in a long time, a mixture of shock, fear, and pain. Then I noticed his teeth, which were glinting even in the dim light. They appeared to be made of metal. Every one of them.

"You've killed her, you son of a bitch," he shouted in German. "Why did you kill our baroness?"

It took me a moment to shift mental gears, but I finally managed to do so. Growing up, most of my friends were Irish, but I was a "Dutchman," as Germans were often called on the east side of Manhattan. Not a tall, blond Teutonic German but a middle-sized, dark-haired German. I do, however, have blue eyes. And because a lot of German was spoken at family gatherings—when I had a family—as well as in the streets, people tell me my accent is tolerable. For an American.

"I didn't kill her," I shouted back, as confused as I was angry. He was bigger than I but looked emaciated. I figured I could take him if necessary. Except for the shotgun he was pointing at me.

"Who the hell are you?" he screamed, shaking the gun at me. "Where did you come from? Why are you here?"

I looked again at the gun and decided to try reason, despite the almost mad fury that filled the fellow's face. "Look! Her blood is already dried, and I just walked through that door two minutes ago. I arrived at this island half an hour ago. My boat is anchored down in that cove."

"You came to rob us. To rape our baroness. You walked in that door and killed her with that ax."

I looked at him, whoever he was, and wondered if maybe *he* had killed her, whoever she was. I couldn't see any blood on him, but he might have cleaned up. Then I looked at the gun. It was still pointed right at my gut, and he was clenching it tightly with both hands. Could I take it from him? I doubted it. My first attempt at reason and logic hadn't achieved much, but I had no choice except to give diplomacy another try. I looked at the gun again. "Look," I said with the most pleasant smile I could force onto my face, "I didn't kill this woman."

"She was our mistress and our lover. She was our life. She was our baroness. Demanding but adorable. We were a happy family, Ilse, Ernst, and I." His eyes filled with tears, and he looked like a man who had just lost everything he ever valued. I didn't know how to respond.

"Who are you?" he asked.

"My name is Frederick Freiman."

"German?"

"No, American."

"You're a lying shit." The tears had disappeared, replaced by a snarl as he rammed the gun barrel into my side, then pulled it back. I lunged for the barrel but was too slow and received another vicious stab at my kidney. Stumbling back, I couldn't take my eyes and mind off his gleaming, pewter-colored teeth.

"I must find Ernst and tell him. You, march!" As he spoke he waved the gun toward an opening in the wall that led into what proved to be the kitchen. The space was far from grand but totally adequate for its function: stone walls, a big porcelain sink with a single faucet connected to a pipe that disappeared through the wall, a black, cast-iron stove and oven, and several long wooden tables and storage chests. Each surface had been scrubbed to within an inch of its life. "Pick that up," my host shouted, waving the gun in the direction of a wooden trapdoor set into the floor.

I could guess where this was leading, and my throat, dry as cinders now, began to clamp shut. "Water, please." I had to struggle to get it out.

"Open it, shithead!"

I bent down, grabbed the ring in the center of the door, and lifted. In front of me lay a dark hole that I assumed was some sort of root cellar or cool storage pit. I had started to lay the door down when the shotgun's butt slammed into the side of my head. Even before the pain could blossom fully I felt myself kicked forward. I fell, knees first, through the hole, only to come to a bone-crunching stop almost immediately. Fortunately, I didn't land directly on either knee, although both legs and my side were badly bruised. The bruises were nothing, however, in comparison with the Fourth of July horror inside my skull.

Before I could recover my wits and take even one breath, the door slammed down and I was surrounded by total, absolute darkness. I tried to stand but vomited instead, barely aware of the crashing and scraping as my jailer moved something heavy over the door. Shuddering, clutching my head, and on the verge of screaming, I lay there for some time. Later, much later, my brain began to work again. I forced myself to stand and pushed up on the door. It was there to stay. I sat down hard on the rough floor and found myself focusing on the throbbing pain in my side and legs. I managed to stand again, and again tried the trap. As I already knew, I wasn't going anywhere soon.

2

This, my first acquaintance with the fabled and tortured Galápagos Islands, occurred on a warm, dry late October afternoon. It was 1938 and World War II was exploding to life. Hitler had already wrapped his arms around Austria and was in the process of doing the same to the Sudetenland. Back in the Fatherland, he was busy building concentration camps and filling them with political opponents, Communists, Gypsies, Jews, and just about everybody else he didn't like. And on the other side of the Pacific, in Asia, the Japanese were equally busy beating the crap out of every Chinaman they could get their hands on. Based on what I'd read in the newspaper, the world was a mess, although many Americans seemed totally unaware of it. I, however, was certain it was just going to get worse. Dire though the world's prospects seemed at the time, mine seemed only marginally better. My discovery of Las Encantadas, as the Galápagos are sometimes known, was a godsend. Or so it had seemed at first.

I'd set out from New York three months earlier in an old forty-foot ketch named *Pegasus*. I'd told everybody I'd met since leaving Sheepshead Bay that I wanted to prove I was

just as tough and salty as old Joshua Slocum, the first man
to sail single-handedly around the world. Not quite as tough,
I guess, since I planned to use the Panama Canal rather than
suffering all the way around Cape Horn. But that explanation
was a lie. I'd left New York because it was a very, very good
time for me to get out of town. I'd left because if I hadn't,
I'd have been dead within weeks, if not days.

The first leg of the trip, from New York south around
Florida and on to Panama, had gone swimmingly. Once I'd
made it through the canal, though, everything began to
fall apart. The engine overheated and cracked. I considered
turning back but was certain that the less time I spent in
places where American English was spoken, the longer I
would live. *Pegasus* and I continued on toward Tahiti. The
next day the radio died of saltwater poisoning. And then
everything really went to hell. Vicious squalls attacked day
and night, drowning me in rain and saltwater and driving me far south of my intended track. When the weather
let up, the wind died. As I drifted, inscrutable ocean currents and countercurrents carried me south and east, then
west, then south into the Doldrums, those windless regions
where, according to fable, ships can be trapped for eternity.
I became merely a passenger, utterly powerless to control
the boat's movements.

Days passed and soon became weeks. Many weeks. What
do people who sail alone over long distances think about? The
wind, the waves, how fast the boat is leaking, and how much
food is left. I also thought, hour after hour, about what I'd left
behind and where I'd really like to be at the moment. And
how hard they might be looking for me, and what they'd do
to me when they found me. And I worried about whether
Uncle Alf would ever forgive me.

Six weeks after I passed through the Panama Canal, I was down to a couple gallons of thick, green, organic water that didn't improve in flavor even after being filtered through an old shirt. I knew I couldn't last much longer. I sat in the cockpit hour after hour and stared out at the limitless Pacific. A pair of porpoises appeared, one off each side, blew, and swam past. Not even they could, or would, help me. I didn't want to die at all, but if I was going to I wanted to die fighting. I resented having to wait for it, sitting and doing nothing. Then I spotted a smudge on the horizon to the northeast. "Oh my God!" I gasped, after I convinced myself it wasn't just a freak cloud. It had to be one of the Galápagos, because there was nothing else for hundreds of miles. *Pegasus* continued ghosting through the dark-blue waters of the Pacific, driven by a light breeze from the northwest under a cloudless sky as blue as the water.

I lashed the wheel and went below to celebrate my salvation with a cup of warm, green-tinted water. I tried to sleep but couldn't, so I spent most of the night pacing around the deck, willing *Pegasus* to move faster, faster. Although the boat and I were almost precisely on the equator, the air and the water were cool, thanks to the north-flowing Humboldt Current, born in the Southern Ocean around Antarctica.

I wasn't the first navigator to stumble on the Galápagos by accident. Or to miss them the same way. The sixteenth- and seventeenth-century Spanish first called them Las Encantadas, the enchanted ones. The islands are separated from the Ecuadorean mainland by the vast, trackless expanse of the faceless Pacific Ocean, a plain whose only road signs are the ever-changing waves. Thanks to the confusing ocean currents and the lousy navigational practices of the times, Las Encantadas were never found where the early, imprecise charts said they should be. Many a frustrated navigator concluded that they were figments of somebody's imagination—or works of the devil himself.

The morning after I spotted land, I found the sun hidden directly behind a towering black mass I tentatively identified as Floreana Island. As the orb rose, its rays wrapped themselves around the island's volcanic cone, driving away the heavy, lingering shadows and slowly turning the mountain a brilliant dark green higher up and a pale green-tan at the base. Crowning the peak was a wispy white cloud that looked as if it had been snagged while drifting past.

I hurried below to check the chart again. The island was essentially round and about six miles across, and the water along its edge was far too deep for anchoring. But there was some sort of indentation, a harbor or cove, along the southern side. I turned *Pegasus*, and we glided through the almost flat, impossibly blue water, as I enjoyed what at the time I thought was a victory breakfast—a small can of baked beans. Two hours later I reached the mouth of the little cove and guided the boat in, the boom creaking in the light wind and gentle swells.

I've always liked to believe that I have a good sense for the presence of danger—and evil, if you will—but on this occasion that sense seemed to have deserted me.

The entrance to the cove was narrow and bracketed by high, black stone cliffs, which were adorned with only the faintest hints of vegetation. The air was filled with noisy clouds of seagulls and black-and-orange frigate birds. The cove itself was as almost perfectly round as the island, bordered by beaches of stony black and brown sand. Behind the beach the land rose gently, dressed at first in spare, dry, tangled scrub. By the time *Pegasus* had glided two hundred feet into the cove, the wind had totally died, blocked by the island. I looked over the side, expecting to see the deep blue of six thousand feet of water. Instead I found the pale, imperfect, splotchy blue-green of deep but anchorable water. I scurried forward and dropped the hook.

Feeling a surge of relief, I looked around my new haven at the rocky beach and the green-gray tangle of thirsty scrub. Then I looked up and spotted the castle. It was perched on a rise some distance back from the water and appeared to be built of the same black and brown volcanic stone that surrounded it. It didn't appear outlandishly large—not a great deal larger than a three-car garage—but it was striking, in part because it was there in the middle of nowhere and in part because it had a square tower of two or three stories in one corner.

A powerful sense of unreality and foreboding settled over me as I prepared to go ashore, a foreboding overwhelmed by my craving for a glass of clean, clear, fresh water.

3

I sat in the absolute dark of the cellar, half mad from the pain in my head and nauseated by the smell of my vomit. Fortunately there wasn't much, since I hadn't eaten much that morning. I cursed myself and my stupidity for a few minutes. What did the lunatic with the metal mouth have in mind for me? Why hadn't he already killed me if that was the plan? There was no question about one thing—given the chance, I'd kill the bastard. At the very first opportunity.

Trying to think more positively, I pointed out to myself that at least my prison was cool and dry. Bone-dry, in fact. I started exploring using my hands—and my nose. I found several sacks of what had to be potatoes, a mesh bag filled with cabbages, and a variety of other sacks and boxes. Shelves of cans and glass canning jars lined the walls. Sensing salvation, at least in the short term, I knelt next to one of the shelves, grabbed the first jar my hand brushed, and shook it. I could feel a sloshing. Sloshing meant liquid. In a near fury of thirst, I popped the top off the jar and smelled the sharp tang of pickling juice. I set disappointment aside and tried another jar on the next shelf down. Again, sloshing. I opened the top and was rewarded with a fruity, slightly sweet smell. The smell wasn't familiar, but it did seem promising, so I dipped my finger in and tasted it.

Not bad, not bad at all. Not too sweet, a little tangy, and very refreshing. I lifted the jar to my lips and drank the nectar of what I later learned was preserved cactus hips. Refreshed and encouraged, I continued on and found all sorts of preserved fruits—some familiar, some not—along with a row of sauerkraut. I passed on the kraut.

I sat back, almost totally revived, and tried to turn my thoughts to the big picture. Whatever my future held, I wouldn't starve right away. But what about the long term? I crawled over to where I thought the trapdoor was. I crouched and then stood carefully, my hands above my head, until I touched the door. It felt just as solid as before. With a grunt, and some sharp complaints from my bruised legs, I shoved up, and again achieved nothing.

With no way to free myself, my thoughts turned to less attractive topics, like what Uncle Alf was thinking about me. Alf's my only living relative, my parents and younger sister all having died during the influenza epidemic of 1918. I'd managed to avoid their fate by mere luck. Alf, I always figured, had survived because he was a merchant marine officer and had been at sea almost continuously for three years. When my parents died, Alf and Lisl, his wife, had for all intents and purposes adopted me. Because Alf was still at sea a lot, it was Lisl who kept me on the straight and narrow and made sure I paid attention at school.

When Alf finally came ashore and had time for such things, we became very close. Almost father and son. Alf taught me to sail, and he taught me the basics of navigation. Alf had also infected me with the dream of sailing around the world.

Pegasus was Alf's boat, and when Lisl died the boat became the most important thing in his life. Except maybe me. And I'd repaid his kindness by stealing it from him. He'd been out of town when I realized that I had to get out of town myself. I stole his boat and left a short letter that explained nothing. If I'd told him everything, he might not have believed it. If he had believed it, he probably would have started making noise about it and found himself as dead as some people wanted me to be.

It was quiet in the hole. And dark. And the air was thickening. I crouched and pounded with my fist on the trapdoor. Somebody above pounded back with something that sounded as if it would hurt.

"Shut up." In German.

Resigned for the time being, I began to doze off. Aside from Alf there really wasn't anybody else I'd left behind who mattered, except Erin. And, as much as it still hurt to admit it, she was a lost cause.

I had a thing for Erin, and she had one for me. Under other circumstances we'd have married at least two years ago and I'd be a happy father back in Manhattan. But our romance was doomed from the start. Her father, Sergeant McGrath, was one of the top officers in my Hell's Kitchen precinct. Yes, I am, or was, a New York cop. The good sergeant's entire life and being were centered on that precinct house and everything that went on in it. Especially the stuff nobody wanted to talk about. There was, of course, a captain in charge of the precinct and a couple of lieutenants, but McGrath was the real boss. To complete the picture, every other cop in the precinct, except me, was Irish, like Sergeant McGrath. I was "the Dutchman." I was tolerated but never really accepted or trusted. As for McGrath, he didn't even tolerate me. He hated all Dutchmen, even more than he hated the English. After a couple shots of Irish whiskey he'd invariably launch into a rant about the Germans gassing the Allied trenches during the Great War. He insisted he'd been there, although I never saw any proof of that. Whatever the reason for his hatred of Dutchmen, both Erin and I were afraid to defy him. The sergeant could be violent. He'd never hesitated to rough up citizens of all but the loftiest status and even other officers who irritated him. He'd been furious when I managed to get promoted to detective, and he'd made it all too clear that he didn't want a Dutchman in his family.

I awoke to a loud banging and scraping over my head as whatever had been used to hold the trapdoor down was dragged away. A blast of bright light blinded me. "Come out of there, shithead," commanded my jailer.

Dazed, I looked up into the early afternoon light. "Where's the ladder, Ritter?" asked another voice—one I didn't recognize—in German.

"Outside, where it belongs," snapped the familiar voice. "Get your ass out there. Now!"

I managed to drag myself up and out and found a committee of three waiting for me. There was Metal-Mouth, who I now assumed was named Ritter, and a smaller and considerably younger German speaker who I guessed was Ernst. Standing beside them was an Ecuadorean in a wrinkled gray uniform with a revolver holstered at his side and a worried expression on his face. He was average height, much like me, and strongly built—stocky but not really fat. He had a weathered, well-used face that suggested he might be past middle age. At first I assumed he was a soldier or policeman, but there were no insignias or marks of rank or authority on his uniform. He could just as well have been an armed automobile mechanic. Except, of course, I damn well knew he was a soldier or policeman. The situation required it, and his black, rock-hard eyes confirmed it.

"Shithead," snarled Ritter as he stepped toward me, swinging the butt of the gun toward my face.

"That'll be enough, Dr. Ritter," said the Ecuadorean in English, in a quiet voice that belied the searing command reflected in his eyes. By now, his expression had changed from worry to irritation. "If you're charging this man with a crime, then he's my prisoner. Under my control."

I stared at Metal-Mouth and tensed, ready to kill him right then and there if I could. But I couldn't, not with him holding a shotgun and the Ecuadorean carrying a revolver. I struggled to play it smart, to get my fury under control

"Oh for God's sake, Ritter," whined Ernst in German. "Do what he says. Otherwise he'll make very big trouble for us. We should have killed and buried this animal before we radioed for the sergeant." As Ernst spoke, the Ecuadorean looked at him with interest, but his expression suggested a total lack of understanding.

Ritter lowered the gun while I studied Ernst more carefully. He was definitely smaller and younger than Ritter, but he had the same exhausted, almost dominated look about him. And, I thought, once he'd been almost pretty.

"Thank you," said the uniformed Ecuadorean, again in English. "Do you speak Spanish?" he asked, his eyes still hard.

"No, sir," I replied, having learned from an early age to be polite to cops I didn't know. "Only English and some German."

"Very well. We'll continue in English. I'm Sergeant López. I'm what you might call the chief of police under the governor of these islands. Who are you?"

"My name is Frederick Freiman. I'm an American citizen; my passport is on my boat, which is anchored in the cove."

"Yes, I saw your boat. What are you doing in the Galápagos?"

"I was headed from Panama to Tahiti when my engine failed. The wind and the currents did the rest."

"Your boat has NEW YORK painted on its stern."

"Yes, I started in New York."

"I see. It has happened before. Dr. Ritter here says he came upon you bending over the bloody body of Ilse von Arndt. Did you kill Miss von Arndt?"

"Baroness von Arndt," snapped Ritter.

"Of course, Doctor," agreed López without turning to look at the German.

"No, sir, I did not," I replied, thinking this sergeant was one to get right to the point. "I came up from the beach and found her lying on the floor, already dead. Her blood was bone-dry."

López stepped back and looked me over from head to foot. "Is this how you first saw him, Dr. Ritter?" he asked. "Dressed in these same clothes?"

"I found him just as he is, bent over the body of our dear baroness," replied Ritter. Then turning to Ernst, he mumbled in German that López was just another Latin dummy. López didn't appear to notice the aside, although his lip curled ever so slightly. If I hadn't been staring right at him I would never have noticed. And I didn't, at the time, attach any significance to it. My head still hurt too much to permit any but the most basic thoughts and emotions. "And I will testify," shouted Ritter in English. "I will testify."

"And I also," seconded Ernst.

López turned and looked out into the living room, at the body. He then turned back and looked at us. "Do you recognize that ax?" he asked Ritter.

"Of course, it is the baroness's. Ours. We use it all the time."

"Very well," said López after a long pause. "This is a serious charge. I'll take Mr. Freiman back with me in the gunboat to Wreck Bay. The governor will wish to see him. I'll also take the baroness back with me."

"Must you?" whined Ernst. "We demand that we be allowed to bury her right here."

For a second, López looked as if he might hit the little German, but he restrained himself and wiped his hand across his face as if he were tired. Probably tired of Ernst. "We'll take the baroness to the fish cannery so they can keep her in their cold room. I want Dr. Menéndez to examine her."

Ritter looked as if he was about to join the argument, but didn't.

"You two may help the sailors wrap the body, and then have Sofía clean up the mess."

It was only then that I noticed the tiny Ecuadorean woman standing in the corner, half hidden behind the stove. I also spotted the glance of utter contempt that Ernst tossed in her direction.

"You can't take this charge seriously," I sputtered, losing control for a minute as Sergeant López led me out of the kitchen into the living room. "It's insane." Any faint hope I'd had that this was an honest, rational, and competent cop began to melt. I started to demand that he do a proper investigation but then thought better of it, realizing that any professional suggestions might lead to matters I had no desire to discuss. I wondered what sort of jail he ran and just how desperate he was for a quick confession that would allow him to close the case. I also had a sneaking suspicion there might not be a defense lawyer within a thousand miles. I paused for a moment and stared down at the body and its surroundings. The sofa and table were there, as were several other chairs, and the beer bottles were where they had been, but the collection of rocks was gone. My mind noted the fact, but once again it didn't register until much later.

"The governor will decide that. Come."

"He should be in chains," snarled Ritter as the gun in his hands drifted higher.

"He will be, in due course, Doctor," said López, picking up a battered briefcase I hadn't spotted before and turning to go. As I followed the sergeant out the door, I noticed that Ritter was grinding his teeth and still clutching the gun while Ernst smiled smugly.

"We'll go aboard your boat to get your passport," announced López as we reached the beach. A large gray rowboat was waiting there, its two oarsmen lying on their backs on the rocky sand. We pulled out to *Pegasus*, and I climbed aboard. The sergeant followed me and sent the boat back to the gunboat to collect two more sailors to help move the baroness's body. While I retrieved my documents from under the navigation table, López looked around.

"Your engine is a mess," he remarked. "Do you have a pistol somewhere to go with the rifle I see on that bulkhead?"

"I do," I admitted.

"Let me see it."

I dug it out and handed it to him. He studied it for several minutes, then handed it back to me. "We'll leave them here where they'll be safe."

"OK."

"Your name is Frederick."

"Yes."

"Do people call you Fritz?"

"Some do," I admitted, even though I tried to avoid the nickname. I was an American, and Fred was an American name. Fritz wasn't. It was the sort of thing some Irish Mick might call me after too many beers.

"Good. I'll call you Fritz."

Whether or not I like the name, I didn't like the way López said it. There was a sneer in his voice if not on his face. It was his way of putting me down or perhaps establishing that he had total control over me. Control to the point that he would be the one to decide what name I would answer to.

I was beginning to feel as if I were with Alice in Wonderland. Was this cop hopelessly crazy or hopelessly crooked or what? He certainly wasn't the sort of cop I'd expect to run across on an island chain dropped out in the middle of nowhere and inhabited by a couple hundred impoverished fishermen and small farmers. Along with a pack of very strange Krauts. But then what sort of cop *would* you expect to find in a place like this? And maybe he wasn't even a cop. Where was his badge?

With me following, López climbed back up into the cockpit and lit a cigar. We sat for some time, not speaking. "Are you going to throw me in jail?" I asked.

"I don't have a jail. I just have an office in the governor's mansion and a little room there that I live in. When I do have a troublemaker, I turn him over to the navy. The commandant has a few cells." He again lapsed into silence.

The rowboat finally pulled away from the shore. It was badly overloaded with four live sailors and one dead baroness wrapped in canvas. Once clear of the beach, it turned and headed out toward the small, gray navy gunboat that was anchored maybe fifty yards away from *Pegasus*.

"Sergeant," I said very carefully, "my boat isn't anchored in a very safe position. If the wind shifts to the south, it may be driven up on the rocks. Would you allow the gunboat to tow it to a safer location?"

He looked at me a moment. "A very prudent suggestion, Fritz. I see no problem. And I'll leave a sailor here to keep an eye on it until you return. You don't have much food left, but I'm sure Ritter will feed him if I tell him to. They, Ritter and Ernst, are afraid of me."

Without further explanation, López left me aboard *Pegasus* and dropped off a sailor on the beach to retrieve my dinghy and guard *Pegasus*. He then had himself rowed to the eighty-foot gunboat. While the frigate birds drifted through the cloudless sky, watching us and occasionally diving to steal some morsel from the much smaller seagulls, *Pegasus* was towed to a safer location. The beat-up gunboat came alongside again, and I pulled myself aboard. Within a few minutes we were out in open water, headed north toward the islands' administrative center at Wreck Bay, twenty-five miles away. From the sound of the engines, and the clouds of black smoke that trailed astern, I was pretty sure the gunboat's propulsion system was in only marginally better condition than *Pegasus*'s.

4

"Sergeant López," I remarked an hour later, after a late lunch onboard the gunboat of rice, beans, and fried plantains had restored some of my confidence, "do you think I killed that woman?"

He looked at me, then smiled with his lips curled ever so slightly. "No, of course not. If you had you'd be as bloody as she is."

"Is that it?" I couldn't restrain myself. "Is that the extent of your investigation?"

He laughed. "You're a spunky fellow! You aren't a policeman by any chance, are you? Your passport says you're a businessman."

I gasped internally, hoping the paleness I felt within wasn't visible without. "No, I was in the construction business, but now I'm just a sailor. A nosy sailor who worries that he's getting railroaded. You know what that means?"

"I do, and you aren't. What I know about the murder of the Baroness von Arndt is this: She was killed by a hatchet blow to the right side of her head. The attacker was behind her, based on where the hatchet handle was pointed, suggesting that the attacker was right-handed. There were no bloody footprints, suggesting that the attacker pushed his victim forward as, or just after, he struck. Footprints or not, the attacker was probably sprayed with some blood. There were no fingerprints I could find pressed into the dried blood and few surfaces in the room from which I might recover any, including the handle of the hatchet. The murder undoubtedly occurred during the night and right where you found the body. The woman and her love slaves were not popular among either the Ecuadoreans or the foreigners who've settled in our islands the last five or ten years. And it's always possible that Dr. Menéndez may be able to add something. Perhaps the baroness was with child. Who knows? Is there anything I've overlooked?"

"Then why am I in custody?"

"Because the governor wants to talk to you. He's already very upset about this murder. We don't have many here. And now that I know you, I also want to talk to you."

"About what?"

"You'll see."

"These islands are very strange."

"Yes, they're said to be enchanted. For a long time sailors thought they could move around on their own."

"I mean the people."

"The people? We Ecuadoreans are very normal. Poor, hard-working, but normal."

"What about those Germans? Ritter, Ernst, and the woman?"

"Yes, we consider them a little strange. All of them. Many Germans live here now. They've come to escape the troubles in Europe. And there are others, also. French, Italians, English, Norwegians, even Americans. In my opinion they're all fugitives. If you're in the Galápagos and aren't a native, then you're a fugitive. From the law, from your past, or from reality."

"What do you know about the murdered woman and her friends?

"Ah, you are becoming interested in the problem! The baroness and her two lovers arrived about five years ago. They had all the necessary papers from Quito, the capital, to settle and build right where they did. They also had money, a lot of money, so they hired islanders to build that castle, complete with a tower. Then they hired more to take care of it and to wait on them."

"What's in the tower?"

"Nothing that I know of. I think it's there because a castle has to have a tower."

"Was she really a baroness?"

"I assume she was. Quito calls her one. She's from some part of Germany I never heard of."

"And her two friends?"

"All I know about them is that one is a dentist and both loved to be dominated by her. One of the reasons she's unpopular with the other Germans is that when she first arrived she insisted they treat her like a baroness. Most of them came here to get away from that sort of thing."

Unfortunately, López was right—I was becoming interested in the problem and not just because the sergeant, who was the major authority figure in my life at the moment, wanted me to be interested. It was, I realized, a triple mystery—who had killed her, why had they killed her, and who was she, really? "You say she was especially unpopular?"

"Yes, she had many enemies. She was domineering, and nobody likes a domineering woman. She also had a temper and very imperfect morals. You have met two of her lovers. She had others."

"Did she have any friends?"

"None that I know of. Except those two."

López lit his small after-lunch cigar and stared off at the horizon. I guess that's all I'm going to get for now, I thought, looking at San Cristóbal, the tan and black pile of volcanic cinder that lay ahead in the distance.

The sun was well on its way to the horizon and the temperature had fallen to that of an early autumn night in New York when we reached our destination. Wreck Bay may have been the administrative and legal center of the islands, but few Americans would have believed it. There was no main street lined with streetlamps and brick stores, and no county courthouse fronted by columns and overlooking a paved, tree-shrouded square. There was no main street at all, although there was a sandy central plaza of sorts. The settlement was composed of a large cinder block and stone building that served as naval headquarters, and about fifty wooden structures, some roofed with thatch, some with corrugated and rusted metal. Except for the headquarters, all the buildings were built of wooden planks so weathered they might have been driftwood. Many had been erected leaning against each other and were surrounded by low wooden palisades built to keep the pigs from roaming. Or maybe to keep roaming dogs from attacking the pigs. Or the goats. And all was set on a wide, brown beach that was frequently flooded, thanks to the islands' often freakishly high tides.

The gunboat turned into the open-mouthed bay and slowed as it approached the long, rickety wooden pier that connected land and sea. An ancient, rust-streaked coastal steamer had just stopped alongside the dock. A crowd of waving, shouting Ecuadoreans was there to greet it. "That's the boat from Guayaquil," López explained.

The gunboat approached the other side of the pier, which was already partially occupied by a handsome, businesslike launch about forty feet long with a small cabin. A police whistle blew aboard the Guayaquil boat, a short gangway appeared, and a parade of passengers, some holding on to their hats in the stiffening breeze, marched ashore. All were dressed in their best outfits and carried an incredible array of sacks and boxes. The air was filled with loud shouts of welcome and joy. I might not understand Spanish, but I can understand emotion when I hear it. As the new arrivals rushed to embrace their greeters, the ship's two cranes swung into action, swaying everything from furniture to God knows what ashore.

"Ah!" said López, staring at the freighter. "She's returned. And dressed like a foreigner."

I followed his glance, and my eyes settled on a tall, slender young woman wearing loose-fitting pants and a checked, long-sleeved shirt. She was standing on the ship's deck, talking with the captain. "Come," commanded López after the gunboat had been moored to the dock behind the big workboat, "I have to speak with her."

"Who is she?"

"Señorita Ana de Guzmán. Her father, Don Vicente, owns a large plantation on Santa Cruz, in the highlands. He's one of the wealthiest men in the islands, although he only lives here part of the year. He sent her to university in the United States, and we've been told she's here now to learn more about operating the plantation. She's his only child."

"Was she raised here?"

"Partly here and partly on the mainland."

"*Sargento*," said the young woman as we approached. Close up, she was stunning. She had a strong face, yet it possessed a powerful hint of sensuality. It was a vibrant face topped by a knot of light brown hair and dominated by blue eyes that sparked with good humor and a mouth that seemed made to smile.

"Señorita," replied López, nodding. "You've returned to our beautiful islands!" he continued in English. I suppose for my benefit.

"For a while."

"May I present Mr. Frederick Freiman? Mr. Freiman is an American sailor who'll be spending a little time in our islands while his engine is repaired."

"Mr. Freiman," she said, sticking out her hand.

I shook her hand and looked into those sparkling, almost laughing eyes. My visit to the Galápagos might very well prove to be more enjoyable than I'd assumed.

"It's a pleasure to meet you,"

"And how is the mainland?" asked López.

"The poor are still poor, the politicians are determined to kill each other, and everybody's worried about which war will ruin us first," she replied, her smile fading but still hanging on.

"Do people really think the war in Europe will reach here?" I asked, wanting to be part of the conversation.

She studied me a moment. "Definitely an American," she finally said, shaking her head slowly. "The Germans are very busy in South America trying to make friends, but they aren't the only problem. It also looks like we'll have a war with Peru over who owns which scrap of worthless land. And our own country is, as usual, inches from a new civil war. The right, the left, the aristocrats, the labor unions, the big American companies are all maneuvering, trying to either defend or overthrow the current government. And it's not only the Americans. The Germans are up to their necks in it. And so are the British. Right, *sargento?*" She was no longer smiling at all.

"You are correct, señorita.

"I see you've brought your father some presents," continued López, waving toward the steady stream of boxes moving across the pier from the ship to the launch moored ahead of the gunboat.

"Oily gears and strange tools and chemicals and all the other things he so likes." She paused. "I suppose I'll soon learn to love them, too." As she spoke, her smile returned and her eyes seemed to have locked on me. López noticed. "How have all our foreign settlers been behaving?" she asked.

"One of them," remarked López drily, "got herself killed just last night."

"Who?"

"The baroness."

"Ah!" The wind ruffled the señorita's hair. "She wasn't a nice woman. Very strange, in fact. There are all sorts of stories about her." After a pause she continued: "Maybe I shouldn't say that. I've only met her once or twice, briefly. She seemed cold, hard, but all I really have to go on is gossip. They say she has—had—many lovers. Sometimes," she paused, "I wonder if sirens sing their songs intentionally to trap sailors or if they sing because it's their nature to sing."

Another pause followed. "Who did it?"

"I don't yet know who killed her, señorita."

"We all count on you to find the answer, *sargento,*" she replied. "It'll be dark soon. I'm afraid I really must get going. I've got to help Roberto finish loading this stuff." She turned away, then turned back to me. "Perhaps you'll come visit my parents and me. We don't get much new blood out here."

"I'd love to," I managed to get out, hope blossoming within me, the first I'd felt in what seemed like forever. She smiled again briefly and winked, then her businesslike frown reappeared, and she hurried down the gangway and across the pier to superintend the loading of her father's machinery into the well-maintained launch. About halfway across the pier she looked over her shoulder at us, her smile now replaced by a frown that suggested I wasn't totally sure what. Disapproval? Suspicion? Worry? I glanced at López and realized that he was staring at her, a far-from-friendly expression on his face.

The sergeant was not only surprisingly well informed about many things but also clearly rational. He even had a sense of humor of sorts, and he'd saved me from Metal-Mouth. He was a cop, I was a cop. I should have felt a connection. I didn't. I didn't like him, and I didn't trust him. I didn't understand him, either.

5

"A very beautiful woman," I remarked as López led me down the pier toward land. "And, I bet, very smart."

"There are many who think she's too smart. The way she sometimes dresses, the way she talks in public. But then her father is very powerful, and we're becoming accustomed to foreigners and their habits."

"I keep learning things from you."

"Soon you'll be learning things *for* me."

I didn't like the sound of that. "What American university did she go to?" I asked, hoping to change the subject to a more attractive one.

"Is there a Barnard University in New York?"

"Barnard College. It's connected to Columbia University."

"So you both have just come from New York. Perhaps you know some of the same people."

"I doubt it," I answered quickly, certain I was right. I didn't know any college girls from wealthy South American families. All I knew were twisted Irish cops, drunks, bums, thugs, and a couple OK Krauts. And Alf. And Erin. "New York's a very big city."

"Come, Fritz. The governor is waiting."

I followed my keeper off the pier and across the soggy sand toward the stone building.

"Are those really metal teeth in Ritter's mouth?" I asked.

"Yes, stainless steel. He's a dentist."

"A dentist with stainless steel teeth?"

"He learned before he came that he'd be the only real dentist in the islands, so he had all his teeth removed and the steel ones put in. That way he'd never have to worry about having a toothache and nobody to fix it."

López chuckled coldly, and I wasn't really sure whether or not to believe him. But what other explanation could there be? "What about you? Where are you from?"

"Me? I'm a native Galapaguino. Most of us live our entire lives here. A few move to the mainland. Some, like me, leave and then return. I sailed aboard merchant ships for almost thirty years. Both oceans and the Mediterranean. I've been to Rome and London and South Africa and even Hong Kong. You name a port and I've probably been there. Along the way I worked very hard to learn English, because I wanted to know what lies others were telling about me. I learned many, many things. But I never forgot Las Encantadas, so I came back, and the last two governors have asked me to work for them. The navy is really in charge, but they don't want to deal with civilians, and there's very little crime here anyway. Whenever a problem does come up, they let me take care of it."

"And I'm your current problem?"

"Yes. You and the baroness. But there are complications. Both the governor and the naval commandant are concerned. You *are* a policeman, aren't you?"

I tensed. How did he know?

"A New York policeman? Why did you leave New York?"

Of course! It was my revolver. It was a standard-issue snub-nosed revolver. Only cops and crooks carried them.

"All my life I've wanted to sail around the world. So now I am."

"Is that all there is to it?"

"You ask far too many questions around here."

"Just the opposite. We ask very few. Most of the people who live here don't like questions. I only ask because I think you may be able to solve a problem for me so I can concentrate on other matters—Becker!" he suddenly snapped, half to himself, looking to one side with an irritated expression. I followed his gaze to a tall, blond fellow with a ramrod-straight back and a face that looked as if it had been chiseled out of granite. The new arrival was strutting across the sand, dressed in a sharply creased gray cotton shirt and trousers of a military cut. "Señor Becker, I didn't realize you were at Wreck Bay."

"I am here for a very short time, Sergeant, to collect a package from the mainland, and then I will proceed on my business." As he spoke, Becker exhibited the same distaste for López that the sergeant had for Becker.

"Yes, of course," replied López.

The tall German—for what else could he be?—looked me over a moment with coldly dismissive eyes. "López?"

"This is Mr. Freiman. He's an American sailor who's visiting us for a while so he can repair his boat."

"Freiman? American? Are you American or German, Mr. Freiman?"

"American."

"Perhaps. You know we are reshaping Germany and, in time, the world. Will America join us in our crusade to rid the world of Reds and Slavs and other lesser peoples?"

"I have no idea what the United States will do," I replied, not wanting to make any more new enemies. At the same time I was certain, Kraut or not, that he wasn't my kind of guy.

The German continued to stare at me a moment, then turned and marched off toward the pier.

"Another one of your German settlers?" I asked.

"No," replied López in a slightly distracted tone, "he's German, but he's a visitor, not a settler."

As we trudged over the rocky sand, passersby nodded quickly at López or tried to avoid eye contact completely. Very few smiled, and those who did smiled nervously. It was the way people in most places react to cops. Or maybe a little more so. The exception was a half dozen small, raggedy children, no more raggedy, really, than many I'd seen in New York. They were utterly oblivious to him. They were playing a game of soccer on the sand and took no more note of our passing than they did of the falling night.

Suddenly a small but vicious-looking tan-and-white mutt appeared from nowhere, barking and charging. "No, Bobo," said López, leaning over and waving his index finger at the beast. Bobo skidded to a stop, licked his lips, and trotted off, while two sailors, who'd stopped talking to a girl to watch the attack, chuckled. López looked sharply at them, and they quickly returned to romance.

We slogged past a very tired and very small stake truck and then a far-from-impressive old Ford sedan that I later learned was for the commandant's use. When we reached the building, the sergeant held the door open for me and then entered himself. A sailor sitting at a table within stood and stiffened, coming to attention. López said something to the sailor, who turned and hurried down a hall. Meanwhile, the sergeant led me to a spartan conference room and sat at the big, scarred table, indicating that I should do so too. The room was cool, almost cold, and damp. The door opened, and a tall, middle-aged naval officer with a large nose came in. López jumped to his feet and greeted the officer in Spanish, then pointed at me. "This is Mr. Freiman, Commandant." I stood, and the officer looked at me a moment with what I can only describe as a skeptical expression, then nodded and sat down. "The commandant's still perfecting his English," said López to me. López and I sat, and we all looked at each other in silence. There was the taste of tension in the air. At first I assumed it was rooted in the baroness's murder, but then I realized there might be something more. The sergeant and the commandant didn't like each other.

The governor arrived. He was small, thin, and stooped, and dressed in a rumpled white linen suit and tie. He was also surprisingly young, in his twenties I would guess. But his most obvious, and most memorable, characteristic was the overpowering stink of gin that surrounded him and soon filled the room.

"Is this the man?" he asked in English, sitting as López, the commandant, and I all stood.

"Sit down," he ordered with an expression of distaste. "He's the one who murdered the baroness?"

"That's very possible, Your Excellency," agreed López, "but it's also possible it may have been somebody else."

"An Ecuadorean?"

"Again, possible. She was far from popular."

"Another German? One of those perverts she kept as slaves?"

"If it was an Ecuadorean I can find him, Excellency, but I've always had difficulty dealing with the foreigners. Especially the Germans. I don't understand their language, and I'm not sure I understand how they think."

"And you think your prisoner does?"

"Before he took up sailing he had experience investigating crimes. He speaks German; he must have German relatives, so he'll understand how their minds work. I think he'll be able to learn much that I can't."

"It's important that this murder be solved quickly. One way or another. It won't look good for me if it's not. It will make it impossible for me to ever get permission to return to Quito. I'll die in this godforsaken place." The governor bent his head down and clutched his hands, only to raise them to cover his eyes. But not before I noticed his tears. His whole body now quivering, he reached out, snatched a glass of water, and shattered it against the wall, exploding water and glass shards in all directions. The abject despair that flowed from his eyes along with the tears was all but overwhelming.

The commandant eyed the governor and then spoke very slowly in broken English. "The murder of the baroness must be solved, and the criminal caught, but I am much more concerned about the other matter we have discussed. Perhaps this man can work his way in among the Germans and learn what we need to know."

"Yes, he'll undoubtedly be able to help there also, although I would prefer he concentrate on the baroness," insisted López.

"Yes," said the governor.

"We're agreed, then?" concluded López. "Mr. Freiman is to find out who killed the baroness. He's also to learn more about a certain German national who's wandering around our islands."

The governor looked up, his tears still evident. Then both he and the commandant nodded in agreement.

"And if he fails to provide us with what we need, we'll have to send him to the mainland for trial as the baroness's murderer. Ever since the penal colony was closed we've had a reputation as a very peaceful place, and we'd all like to keep it that way."

Once again the governor and the commandant nodded. I looked around the table and realized that none of them were looking at me or even at each other. An overpowering sense of loneliness, and a very sharp sort of fear that I hadn't felt for some time, swept over me. I was totally alone, totally friendless, in a land where I couldn't even speak the language. If I disappeared into some dungeon or just died, nobody would know or care. In a way the scene was horribly comic. Despite the seemingly offhanded way they were discussing my future, they were all totally serious. If I didn't produce a suitable killer, I was as good as dead.

"Are you angry with me, Fritz?" asked López as he led me out of naval headquarters. I just looked back at him, still a little shocked at the way I'd let myself be so neatly skewered and set to roast over a raging fire. And I still didn't like the tone of his voice when he said "Fritz." For a moment—a very brief one—New York almost looked safer than where I was.

"Don't worry, I'm sure you'll succeed. You'll have little trouble learning more than any of us really want to know from the gringos, the foreigners. Most, if not all, disliked, even hated the baroness and her drones, and many dislike each other. They'll want to tell you every bad thing they can think of about each other. They'll tell you things they wouldn't say to an Ecuadorean. You'll fit in. They'll sympathize with you. Do you want a cold beer?"

Yes, I thought. I could very much use a cold beer. Dusk was settling in; the temperature was edging down; the breeze continued to build, gracing the exposed harbor with a notice-able chop; and the air was thickening as an evening haze developed. Despite the cooling I was damn thirsty, my mouth dry from tension, and the sergeant's calculated cynicism did nothing to relieve my discomfort. "Yes, I'd like that."

López, my new employer, so to speak, led me across the settlement's plaza of damp sand, returning the guarded greetings of various passersby, all of whom were barefoot. The men were dressed in long trousers and undershirts and the women in well-worn dresses, most adorned with what had once been bright prints. When we were about halfway across the plaza, a young woman in a splotched dress walked past, eyeing me. She stopped and winked, her smile as wide as she was and her two missing teeth just as obvious. "¡*Que guapo!*" she said, her eyes twinkling in the dim light as she looked intently into mine.

"No, Esme," snapped López, shaking his finger at her with the same expression he'd awarded Bobo, the dog.

"We have a few of those here, Fritz, like everywhere," commented the sergeant after Esme had winked again and continued on, dismissed but not apparently intimidated. "Just like in New York. I keep my eye on them and don't let it get out of control."

"What did she say?"

"She thinks you're a handsome fellow." I can't really say he was smiling as he said it.

A few minutes later we turned into a dim passageway between two weather-stained wooden palisades. The air was filled with the smell of human existence—food, sweat, garbage. It smelled just like Manhattan in the summer, except for the addition of the cloying stench of sizzling coconut oil, the sharp tang of drying seaweed and salt, and more than a whiff of dead marine life. We passed a tiny, tired store and then an open-air workshop in which an almost toothless carpenter was planing a plank by the light of a kerosene lamp. A few steps beyond, López stopped before an unmarked opening in the palisade on the right and pointed for me to enter. I found myself in a small, sand-floored, roofless area filled with three or four rickety tables and perhaps twice as many equally decrepit wooden chairs. Along one side there was a small cooking area—an open grill, a table, and an ancient, shoulder-high icebox—protected by the overhanging corrugated metal roof of the adjoining weather-stained house.

"*Hola, sargento,*" said the little man standing next to the grill. López replied, holding up two fingers as he did. He then gestured for me to sit at the nearest table. There were two other customers, sitting at a table in the corner. The two, both men, looked up at us and quickly looked away. As we waited, I listened to a pig snorting and snuffling someplace close by but not in sight.

"Well, Sergeant López," I said as the proprietor placed two coolish beers in front of us and lit a small kerosene lamp in the middle of the table, "you seem to have trapped me pretty well. If I don't find the baroness's murderer then I'll hang for it." I spoke in a jovial tone but was certain that every word was the literal, awful truth. López was proving to be a very hard man.

"We don't generally hang people for murder in Ecuador, Fritz. Especially when the victim is an unpopular foreigner. Sometimes, if it's political, we shoot them. Otherwise we just send them to prison for a very long time, and our prisons make yours seem like the Plaza Hotel in New York. Unless they're rich and have powerful friends, people often never come out."

"I'm as totally trapped here as your governor seems to feel he is."

"Yes, the governor. He's a very sad case." There was little sympathy in López's eyes as he started to explain. "He's the son of a very important family and entered the diplomatic service. At some point he made an error of some sort and was sent here as punishment. Unfortunately, he's very much a man of the capital—the glittering parties, the glittering ladies, the glittering future—and has been totally unable to come to terms with our way of life here." As he spoke, López turned and glowered at the owner of the place, who'd been floating around us as if trying to eavesdrop. The man hurried back to his kitchen. "He was on his best behavior today," continued the sergeant. "Generally he's too drunk to move or is running around screaming and throwing things. I fear for his sake, and for ours, that he will still be here long after you're free to sail away."

"What makes you think I'll succeed?" I asked, perking up at the optimism in the sergeant's words if not in his expression.

"You speak German and English, and you're not Ecuadorean. And you're a very resourceful fellow; otherwise you'd never have lived long enough to see our shores."

"I could just sail away," I suggested, using my fingertips to delicately explore the big, purple bruise Ritter had pounded into the side of my head and wondering vaguely what else López thought he knew about my past.

"Not without an engine. You're no fool. And we keep an eye on who rides the boat to the mainland."

"You seem to have all the answers."

"No. It's up to you to find them for us."

"It may not take that long. Where were Ritter and Ernst when their mistress was killed?"

"An excellent question. You should ask them."

I thought for a minute about motive; that's always one starting point. Especially if it's obvious. And it looked to me at first glance that the motive must have been passion. A savage anger. Planting a hatchet in somebody's head isn't usually a premeditated act. But there was, of course, another classic motive. "Who owns the castle, Sergeant? Whose name is on the deed? The three of them?"

"I'm certain the grant from the government is to the baroness herself. She'd never share it with others."

"Does she have a will?"

"I've never seen it. You'll have to look for it."

"Relatives?"

"Maybe in Europe. None that I know of here."

"So who'll end up owning the castle?"

"The government, probably. Unless those two degenerates manage to find a very good lawyer in Quito."

"Could she have owed somebody money? Or maybe somebody owed her money. Or there was some sort of financial dispute."

"All possible, Fritz."

"What's this other business?" I asked, changing the subject. "Some mystery German wandering around?"

"Yes, you saw him not twenty minutes ago. Becker. That's what he says his name is, and that's what his passport says. Martin Becker. He's not like the others. We, especially the commandant, want to know who he really is and what he's here for."

"That tall, starchy guy? Marches around like a Prussian general?"

"Yes."

"How's he different?"

"He's clearly not a settler. He just wanders around exploring and talking to people. He says he's a businessman looking
for opportunities, but he never seems to find one he likes."

"Do you think he's involved with the murder?"

"It's possible, anything's possible, but I doubt it. We're
interested in him for other reasons."

"You think he's a spy? War with Germany does seem
almost certain. At least for us."

"That's what the commandant wants you to find out. But
remember, your priority is finding the baroness's killer. That's
highest on the governor's list and we, you and I, work for
him." López then raised two fingers again and called out to
the owner.

I looked at my bottle and realized it was empty. "These
Germans live on different islands?" I asked, returning to the
business at hand.

"Three, for the most part. Here on San Cristóbal, on Santa
Cruz, and Floreana."

"How do I get around? On *Pegasus*?"

"No. You'll be able to get a ride from the navy sometimes,
and it's always possible to hire a fisherman to take you from
here to there. I'll give you some money."

"And where will I live?"

"Many will be eager to offer you a room. Otherwise, you
can live on your boat, which we'll move here tomorrow. If
there's wind you can sail it. If not we'll tow it."

"You've thought this all out."

"I truly wish it wasn't necessary. Now I must go and take
care of other matters. I'll walk back to the navy headquarters
with you, then you make yourself at home there."

With no streetlights and one generator that served only the
naval facility, Wreck Bay at night was dark and shadowy, lit

by the occasional kerosene lamp shining through a window or the flare of a cooking grill. Much as I was growing to dislike and distrust the sergeant, I was a little grateful to have him with me as we walked back through the narrow passages toward the plaza.

After we'd reached naval headquarters, I watched the sergeant climb on an old motorcycle that I hadn't noticed before. What, I asked myself, did López wish wasn't necessary? That he might inconvenience me? No, I'd already pegged him as one hard son of a bitch who wouldn't care in the slightest if he inconvenienced God. It was the investigation itself that he wished wasn't necessary. Somehow it was a threat to him.

I continued to watch as López kicked the bike to life and roared off into the night, headed inland over a sandy track that wouldn't be called a road anywhere else.

I then realized that he'd never bothered to pay for our beers. I'd never seen Sergeant McGrath pay for any, either.

6

Early the next morning I walked along the shaky pier carrying a small case of beer and feeling much better about the world than I had the night before. My head was a bit sore, but a good night's sleep always seems to make the world look a lot better. And I was on my way to do something positive—reclaim my boat. Alf's boat. Best of all, I was going to be free, at least for a while, of López, whose company had already become oppressive.

I stopped beside the gunboat and turned to watch as a familiar launch pulled alongside the dock. The boat was skippered by the same thin, hard-looking Ecuadorean with a revolver at his hip that I'd seen the day before. He was old, I thought, but still looked and acted very fit. I spotted Ana de Guzmán standing next to the skipper, dressed in dungarees and a white blouse with a tan jacket under her arm. She studied me a moment, then waved. I waved back and waited.

"Good morning, Miss de Guzmán," I greeted her as she jumped from the launch to the pier. Life really was looking up! Unless she was about to tell me to go to hell.

"Good morning, Mr. Freiman. Is the navy loaning you their boat so you can do a little sightseeing while your engine is repaired?" she asked with a twinkle in her eye.

Damn it, she was playing with me! "No, I've agreed to help Sergeant López find whoever killed the baroness. I'm off to talk to various people."

"Why did he recruit you, an outsider?"

"He says because I'm an outsider. He thinks people, especially the foreigners, will tell me more than they'll tell him."

"And because you were a New York cop, right? Before you took up sailing around the world. And because you found the body, so he can always say you did it if you can't find who really did."

"How do you know all this?" I was beginning to find her game irritating as hell, and my expression must have shown it.

"I'm sorry," she said, reaching out and touching my forearm gently. "I'm being childish. Roberto told me. Navy sailors have big ears, and big mouths, and some understand a little English. Plus it's a small settlement, and everybody knows just about everything," she explained, nodding at the skipper as she spoke.

"And Roberto knows everybody?"

"He's been in the islands most of his life. He arrived as a prisoner when there was a penal colony here and stayed when his sentence ended. Now he's Papa's launch captain, among other things, and sometimes my bodyguard. I don't really need one, but I don't argue since Roberto and I work well together."

"Does he know who killed the baroness?"

"I don't think so, but I'm sure there's somebody who does. In addition to whoever really did it. There's always somebody, isn't there?"

"Almost always," I replied, hoping I'd find that somebody damn soon. "You and Roberto seem to spend a lot of time riding around in that launch."

"Yes, everybody in Las Encantadas does. We're constantly going from island to island for some reason or other."

"What are you up to today?"

"Picking up some tobacco seeds from a friend of my father's. He has a farm on the mountain a few miles from here. He and Papa are trying to develop a new strain of tobacco, one milder than the horrible stuff we grow here now."

Cigarettes, I thought. I used to smoke them, but I'd run out so long ago I couldn't remember what they tasted like, although López's cigar had been pleasant. From the smell of her breath, I wouldn't be able to mooch any from Ana if I did decide to take up smoking again.

"So your father isn't the only person who likes to tinker with things around here."

"Half the people here tinker in one way or another. It's part of surviving on the edge of the world." As she spoke, there was a gleam in her eyes. Pride, I guess. And perhaps wonder.

What a fascinating, irritating, and beautiful woman, I thought, as I felt a tingling sensation all over. Like practically everybody in New York, I'd always imagined South American princesses as lofty, distant beings from another world. Ana looked the part but didn't seem to play it unless it suited her convenience. I knew damn well what I liked about her but wondered what she could possibly see in me. Maybe it was just that I was a new face. I glanced toward the gunboat and spotted the skipper frowning at me. "I'd better move along," I said, "but I'd really like to see you again. How do I get hold of you?"

"If you don't see me or Roberto wherever you are, ask the navy to radio me at Papa's plantation on Santa Cruz. We use radios here like telephones. And let me warn you—I know all about New York cops."

"What?"

"One night I was out with some friends. The men got very drunk, and we all got arrested." She was laughing again.

"What happened?"

"Nothing, really. The girls weren't drunk, and the boys were all from important families. It was just like here, on the mainland, although we all did get lectures from various deans, and the boys were fined. In my opinion the boys would have benefited from a day or two in jail. They made quite a mess."

I gave her my best cop frown.

"I learned my lesson," she assured me. "Now we both better get going."

"Yes. I hope to see you again."

"So do I."

I watched her walk down the pier, then turned back toward the gunboat.

"Good morning, Mr. Freiman," said a young sailor who was standing next to the gunboat's gangway.

"Good morning," I replied.

"I'm Seaman Rojas, sir. Sergeant López has left word that I'm to be your translator." His English was hesitant at first but totally clear and understandable. Was he the one who'd blabbed about my being a cop?

"Where's the sergeant?" I asked as I stepped aboard.

"He didn't tell me, sir."

López was certainly on his toes, I thought as the gunboat backed away from the dock. Thinking one step ahead. And he's still with me, I added darkly to myself, even though he's nowhere in sight.

As we approached Floreana later that morning I pondered the contrast between the bone-dry shore and the ring of damp, gray clouds that now crowned the not-so-ancient volcano. We pulled alongside *Pegasus* and found the sailor who'd been assigned to look after her practically beside himself with worry.

"He says there was a lot of shouting ashore last night, sir. At the castle. And then there were gunshots. Many gunshots," reported Rojas after he'd listened to the sailor's excited explanation.

"Did he go see what was happening?" I demanded, knowing I wasn't going to like whatever Rojas told me.

"No, sir. He didn't think he should go ashore and investigate. His orders were to take care of your boat."

"When? When did he hear it?"

"Late at night. Maybe early in the morning."

I took a deep breath. I could understand how the sailor felt. If he'd wanted to charge into gunfights, and face the dead bodies that generally resulted, he'd have joined the army. Or the NYPD.

I groaned inwardly. López already had me hard at work even though he probably didn't know it yet. I glanced at the gunboat skipper. He looked very uneasy. I turned to Rojas. "Ask the sailor if he could tell what language they were shouting in."

"It wasn't Spanish, sir," reported Rojas. "He thinks it was German, although it could have been English."

I nodded, not sure if there was any significance to the sailor's answer, then asked Rojas to suggest that the skipper accompany us—Rojas and me—ashore to investigate. The petty officer looked away. I told Rojas to remind him that he was the highest-ranking Ecuadorean official within many miles. The skipper looked back at me coldly and nodded in reluctant agreement. He didn't like being told what to do, especially by a foreigner who couldn't even speak his language. I'd managed to make another enemy.

I retrieved my revolver from *Pegasus*, and we rowed ashore. There I led my reluctant companions up the path to the castle. The air was filled with the faint perfume of sun-baked rocks and seaweed, and all was silent except for the occasional rustle of lizards or the drab little finches. I stopped on the patio and looked in the darkness behind the still-opened double doors, the hair on the back of my neck beginning to prickle. "Hello?" I shouted, hoping that the presence of the two sailors would somehow prevent Metal-Mouth from blowing me to pieces. "Ritter? Ernst?" The only answer was the whispering of a gentle gust of wind in the dry shrub around us. In we go, I thought with teeth clenched and revolver raised.

I stepped through the double doors and found bloody chaos. Much of the elegant, polished furniture had been shattered, its fragments spread all over the room. The baroness's body was gone, safe in the ice factory, but what was left of Ritter and Ernst now lay in her place, Ritter's teeth gleaming slightly through the blood. The walls and floor, which Sofía had been told to mop, were thickly spattered with a whole new harvest of almost-dried blood. The flies were having a field day.

There was a gasp behind me. I turned in time to see Rojas and the gunboat skipper back slowly out the door, shock written large on their faces. Grasping the revolver even tighter than before, I examined the wreckage more closely. Everything that had been there yesterday—the sofa, the coffee table, the chairs—was still there, although most of the chairs had been smashed. The white curtain lay on the floor, and the sofa was toppled over on its back. Nothing seemed to be missing. But was there anything new? The bodies, of course, the blood, and four shotgun shells. The lingering scent of burnt black powder. And the dimples in the walls created by a shot that had missed its target. There were also two beer bottles, one broken at the neck. Were they new, I wondered, or left over from the night before? I lifted one of the bottles and looked in through the neck. A few drops of beer flowed from side to side as I shook the bottle. Sofía had done her job the day before. These bottles were new.

My nerves were ready to burst into flames as I walked across the great room and into the kitchen. Nothing. No blood, and everything was in its place. I lifted the door to my former cell and lowered myself into it. It appeared to be just as it was when I left it—including the stench of vomit— except I could now see that a very large brown spider lived in one corner. I hadn't noticed him during my last visit. I looked carefully at the jars and cans and bundles of food. Was there anything else I'd missed before? Like a metal box of some sort? A money box, maybe? Not that I could find.

I took a deep breath, pulled myself up and out of the pit, and returned to the great room, then followed the house's one hallway, which ran to the back of the building. On the left I found a small, nondescript bedroom with a simple metal bed, a chest of drawers, a wardrobe, and a chair. On the right was a rudimentary bathroom with shower, toilet, and sink. No more bodies, and no blood.

I continued down the hallway and through a curtain. In front of me was the biggest bed I'd ever seen in my life. And just about the grandest. It was an old four-poster with a green canopy and was covered with pillows of all sizes, shapes, and colors. On each side, on the thickly carpeted floor, was a small mattress. And the room itself, which was almost as large as the whole front of the castle, was a wonder. There were three large windows, four chests of drawers, two wardrobes, and a huge mirror. Half a dozen expensive-looking wall hangings depicting forest scenes brought life to the room. There were two doors in the rear. One led out to a small patio and the other into a bathroom—complete with a tub and a large vanity—every bit as ornate as the bedroom.

So this, I thought, is how a baroness maintains her dignity, and maybe her memories, out in the middle of nowhere. Despite her unfavorable reputation, my suspicion grew that the woman was a great deal more complex than I'd been told. She'd chosen to voyage to the end of the Earth, to a rough-and-tumble place with few luxuries, and yet she'd created this little nest that spoke loudly of the refined world she'd probably left. Was she just one more fugitive, or had she come because she believed the islands would provide the freedom to create, or live, some very personal vision? She was dead, so I'd never get to know her, but if I was to find her killer, I did have to understand her. And, to be honest, I wanted to.

I searched the suite again. No blood. Nothing that seemed out of place. Nothing, as far as I could tell, except that the huge bed was unmade. It looked as if a war had been fought in it. Sofía, the maid, had been all too efficient at cleaning up after the baroness's death. Fortunately for me she hadn't yet set to work today. I doubted she would, for that matter. Who was left to pay her?

On the assumption that I couldn't foul the crime scene any more than I already had, I opened each of the chests of drawers. In the top drawer of one, mixed in with the clothes that jammed them all, I found a lacquered wooden box with its lock smashed open. Inside were three passports and a formal-looking document several pages long.

The first passport I opened was Metal-Mouth's: Wilhelm Conrad Ritter, Doctor of Dentistry, born December 1899, in Cologne. The second belonged to Ernst Friedrich Lang, occupation not given, born March 1909, in Dortmund. Finally, Bettina Ilse Judith von Arndt, housewife, born April 1906, in Aachen.

I flipped through the official document. It was in Spanish, so Rojas would have to tell me what it was.

Glancing back into the box, I realized there were five or six photographs on the bottom, where they'd been hidden under the document. The first showed a well-dressed man and woman, both smiling, standing in front of a palatial stone house that had a round tower or turret of some sort on one side. To my eye it looked very German, or at least European. Between them was a young girl, dressed in a dirndl, with a huge and very convincing smile on her face. In the second photo the same girl was grinning from the back of a carousel horse. The girl in the photographs had to be the baroness and the adults her parents. And unless I was a total fool, her childhood had been a happy one. I continued to leaf through the photos. Another shot of her as a child, in the mountains. Then the tone changed radically. The next shot showed the same girl, to all appearances a teenager now, standing in a barren, treeless street with a tenement behind her. She was wearing a long, dark overcoat, her shoulders were hunched, and her smile was as frigid as the street itself appeared to be. The final photo had been mutilated. It showed the baroness standing beside a very fat uniformed man, but it was impossible to see the man's face because something, a pen or pencil

I guessed, had been shoved through it. And the smile on her face was more of a sneer.

So the baroness *did* have a past, after all. What had happened? How had the girl with the winning grin become the arrogant, domineering creature that López had described to me?

Other than the passports, the photographs, and the document, there was nothing else in the box. No letters, no other keepsakes of any sort, no hints of why the baroness and her two attendants were in the Galápagos, how they'd met nor what they'd done before they came. Each of them must have had a history, but they appeared to have tried, with considerable success, to leave them behind. On the other hand, there was no money in the box, either, even though it looked to me like exactly the sort of place a baroness might keep her ready cash when there were no banks within seven hundred miles.

I stepped back into the hall and noticed a ladder attached to the rear wall of the building. It led to a trapdoor in the ceiling. It could only be one thing: the tower. I shook the ladder to test its stability and started up. When I reached the trapdoor I pushed it open and found a small, dim chamber. I waited a moment for my eyes to adjust, then pulled myself up and found another ladder leading up to another trapdoor. Once through this second door, I stepped out onto the top of the tower, which was surrounded by a four-foot parapet.

The blue-green bay and the bluer Pacific sparkled in the sun while the black-brown beach baked. The cliffs glowered, the gulls and frigate birds soared and wheeled and screeched, and the green forest stretched off toward the mountain, its color getting richer as it approached the volcano. At first, the only visible evidence of man-made order was the crude geometries of the two gardens. I leaned over the parapet and stared down into the surrounding scrub. There was no sign of anything that might be called a road, although several paths led away from the castle. Following one of the paths with my eyes, I spotted a small building about a quarter mile away in the direction of the mountain. I looked around at the platform and the parapets. Nothing. No sign that anybody had ever been here. And there was nothing of interest inside the tower as I descended again.

Who was the Baroness Bettina Ilse Judith von Arndt, really? Who had killed her and her lovers, and why?

7

I returned to the great hall and reexamined the bodies, the bloody walls, and the floor, looking for something, anything, to give me a direction. Each of the Germans had been blasted several times at very close range. There were no foot- or handprints in the blood, although it was clear that at least one of the victims had tried to crawl or twist through the mess on the floor. I looked for the weapon but couldn't find any trace of it. Neither was there any trace of Ritter's shotgun, so maybe it had been the instrument of his death.

In death, the metal-mouthed dentist looked just as vicious as he had in life, and Ernst looked just as inconsequential. I had no intention of mourning either for so much as a second, but their bloody deaths, on top of the baroness's, scared the hell out of me. Was this the beginning of something truly monstrous, or was it all just a figment of my imagination, a manifestation of the dark enchantment the early navigators believed wrapped the islands? Of course not. It was just a series of murders that could be explained in some logical, matter-of-fact way. Somebody had cheated somebody else and paid for it, or somebody had hated somebody beyond all reason. Or maybe had just been infuriated by him—or her. Or maybe it had been simple armed robbery. That was something I was quite familiar with.

"Rojas," I shouted over my shoulder, "have you recovered yet?"

My translator appeared in the doorway, pale but alive. "The skipper and I think we've found blood out on the patio. Please come look." I followed him out onto the patio, where I found the petty officer staring at the ground. I bent down to get a closer look where he was pointing, at some small brown spots. I dropped down to my hands and knees and followed the faint trail of dried blood back through the double doors until it merged with the disturbed stains on the floor of the great hall. In the dim light it was difficult to follow, but possible. I returned to the patio. "Where does this go?"

We all got down on our hands and knees and followed the brown spots across the patio, only to lose them in the surrounding mix of sand and rock. I straightened up and looked around. The blood trail didn't seem to lead to the beach but rather off to the side, probably toward the dry shrubbery beyond. I thought of the paths through the bush that I'd seen from the tower. And the building. The baroness was undoubtedly wealthy enough to own an automobile, but I didn't see one, and I hadn't seen anything resembling a road. I sniffed the air. "Have you seen any horses, Rojas?"

"No, sir."

There must be some, somewhere, I thought. The building out back must be the barn.

Before forgetting to do so I handed the document to Rojas. "What's this? Can you translate it?"

It took him several minutes to read it through. "It says the government is giving some land—this land, I guess—to the Baroness Ilse von Arndt."

"Only the baroness?"

"Yes, sir. There are no other names here."

I looked in at the bodies. I hadn't seen any large carnivores in the area, except for humans, but I was certain there was an army of smaller ones. Rats, for example. No matter where you go you find rats. And ants. I closed the doors, hoping that would at least help preserve the evidence. "Follow me."

The gunboat skipper said something to Rojas.

"May I ask, sir, where we're going?"

"There's a building over there," I replied, pointing toward the forest. "It must be a barn."

Rojas translated, and the petty officer nodded.

Now all I had to do was choose which of the three visible paths to follow. I looked behind me and up at the tower and tried to remember which way I was facing when I'd spotted the structure. "This one," I said, choosing the one that appeared most heavily used and most likely to lead in the right direction. I pulled my pistol from my trouser pocket, where it had been riding very uncomfortably, and checked its load.

I dove into the thin brush, and the wind seemed to disappear. By the time I'd taken two dozen steps my clothes were soaked with sweat, and an army of flies—horseflies, not houseflies—were already ripping large mouthfuls of flesh from my head and exposed arms. I glanced back at the two sailors. They were better protected by their long sleeves and hats, but they were still far from immune.

We all smelled the barn before we saw it. It turned out to be far from grand—big enough for a horse or two and little more. Along two sides were pens that had probably housed pigs or goats. I approached with my pistol at the ready, the finches screeching and twittering in the trees around us while other creatures—little lizards, mice, I don't know what—scurried over the leaf-covered ground.

"There's nobody here, sir," observed Rojas after we'd looked around.

Not a soul, I thought. And no animals, either. There was evidence that some sort of cart had been there, but it wasn't now. There'd clearly been at least one horse, but it was gone, along with whatever tack had been here.

"Could it have been a robbery?" I mumbled, thinking both of the missing animals and the opened box in the baroness's room. "Could they all have been killed for their possessions?"

"Sir?"

I turned to Rojas. "Could somebody from around here have killed the baroness and the two men in order to steal their animals and whatever valuables might have been in the house?"

"I don't know, sir. I'm only your translator."

I looked at him. The kid wasn't stupid; he clearly had some sort of education.

"Damn it, don't be foolish. You know much more about the locals than I do. You must have an opinion, and I want it."

Surprise appeared on his face, then a wave of anger washed across it only to fade away. There definitely was more to Rojas than I'd realized at first. Which was good, since he was my only contact with the new and nerve-racking world around me.

"I don't think so, sir. The local people might kill if they were insulted badly enough, and they might steal, but they wouldn't kill to steal. I think once they realized both the baroness and her two men were dead they took the animals.

People here are poor and wouldn't see any reason to leave anything for the government to take."

"Thank you, Seaman Rojas." I wondered if a hundred years from now the Ecuadoreans of Floreana would be celebrating the day of the baroness's death as a sort of secular Christmas.

"Did you see that other building over there, sir?" asked Rojas, pointing off to the right at a weathered shack set back in the scrub. I followed him over to the small structure. It had one room and three screened windows. Like the barn, it was built of wood. And it had been stripped just as clean. I carefully sorted through the little that was left—two wooden bed frames, a few magazines, and some scraps of paper—but they told me nothing except that whoever lived here turned to girlie books for solace.

I looked overhead and spotted the sun through the leaves. It was still morning, late morning, anyway. As every cop knows, the sooner you get on the trail of a criminal the better chance you have of catching him. I just had to find the trail. I started to work my way along the side of the shack, scanning the brush and the ground, and alert for any hint of a shotgun pointed in my direction. Despite the cool air and the breeze, I was sweating thinking about shotguns. There was no evidence here of the blood trail, although I was still able to spot places where the ground had been scuffed. Was it the murderer, or just the locals making off with their booty? I followed the scuff marks across the open area to a trail that led into the brush.

"Do you have any idea where this goes?"

Rojas consulted the petty officer.

"He says there's a small settlement on the other side of the island. And some farms on the side of the mountain. He's landed on the beach at the settlement a few times but never really been ashore and never to the farms inland. He thinks it probably leads around the mountain to the settlement."

"Then we'll find out," I announced as I jogged toward the brush.

I continued on, despite the intense irritation evident on the skipper's face, and was soon vaguely aware that the land wasn't sloping up as I'd expected. I stopped to look and realized that we weren't headed inland, toward the mountain, but were running roughly parallel to the shore. Whatever the growing personal discomfort, and the nagging fear of ambush, I was determined to continue. I had to pick up the killer's trail before it became hopelessly cold. About a mile later, the path split. I looked behind us. The castle was long out of sight. I evaluated the choices, swatting wildly at the meat-eating insects as I did, and considered asking my companions' opinions. That, I assured myself, was a waste of time. They'd have no more idea than I did. The right branch, I guessed, must lead down to the shore while the other must continue on around the mountain. After mentally tossing a coin, I turned onto the path to the right. Within another half mile we jogged out of the bush onto a small, rocky beach that looked out over the Pacific.

"Here, Mr. Freiman," called Rojas a few moments later. I trotted over and saw the gouge in the sand where a boat's bow had been pulled up.

"So he, or they, used a boat to get away," I mused aloud. A pair of black-green marine iguanas sunned themselves on a rock outcrop and watched silently. Ugly, hostile beasts, I thought, with their scales and hard eyes and the ridge of long spikes that ran along their spines. They were almost three feet long, and their expressions said that if they were only a little bigger they'd consider having me for dinner.

I looked up and out over the water again, and my hopes of progress evaporated. There, bobbing so very gently in the tiny waves, were a dozen foot-long sections of tree trunk. They were anchored, I realized, and must be marking some sort of trap—for fish or maybe lobster. So the fact that somebody had pulled a boat ashore here within the past few days meant nothing.

Despite the faint breeze, I was hot. Rojas was hot. The petty officer was hot. And we were all parched. I watched the two of them splash saltwater on their faces and necks and followed their example. Even the sting of the salt on the bug bites felt refreshing. The temptation to turn back was almost overwhelming, especially since I could see mutiny boiling in the petty officer's eyes. But if I didn't find the baroness's murderer I'd spend the rest of what would undoubtedly be a short life in a house of horrors on the mainland. "We continue," I said to Rojas. "It'll start getting cooler soon."

"But sir, we're thirsty!"

"Yes, but we must continue."

Rojas started to speak to the petty officer, but the skipper wasn't really listening. His eyes flared with fury, and he strutted toward me, reaching down for a rock with very sharp edges as he did. I reached for the revolver in my pocket. He saw my movement and straightened up without the rock. Bitter resentment still oozed from his eyes, but the determination to attack appeared to have evaporated. I turned and led the way back along the path until we reached the junction and headed up the branch not taken.

Within a few minutes we were marching uphill and my two companions were falling even farther behind. In fact, they were out of sight, hidden by a thick patch of brush. I stopped a moment to let them catch up. Alone again, I thought, in a place I don't understand.

But I wasn't alone. There was something, somebody in the brush off to my left. I could hear it and feel it. I could imagine that damn shotgun pointed right at me. I squatted down and raised my revolver. It was either that or running like hell and getting a back full of shot. At first I saw nothing more than sun-dappled leaves and branches. Then there was motion, a large, gray-brown mass in among the gray-brown-green undergrowth. Sweat ran down my neck and back. I tensed, desperate to locate my target and fire.

The mass moved and became more defined. It looked like a horse. Or a caricature of one. As my mind caught up with my eyes, I could see the creature's head; it was chewing on the sparse leaves. Only then did I recognize it as a mule. Or maybe a jackass. A very big one.

I heard heavy breathing behind me and spun instinctively. It was Rojas. "That's one big burro, sir. A wild one. They're all over the islands. Somebody brought them here sometime, and they ran away. There are also many wild goats and pigs." He was staring at my drawn pistol as he spoke. For some reason he seemed on the verge of laughing, prevented only by his shortness of breath.

I looked back at the beast and stood up. Was Rojas laughing at me, at the near-panicked expression on my face, or was he laughing at the ass? "We have to keep moving. Where's the petty officer?"

"He's coming along, sir. We're both very thirsty."

"So am I," I snapped. "We're bound to find water some-place around here."

"Yes, sir."

As we climbed, the slope continued to steepen. Up ahead, and off to one side, I spotted a small hummock of ten-foot-high palmettos. Then another. Within another fifteen minutes of steady marching, we'd climbed a couple hundred feet and the vegetation was much greener and thicker, the soil distinctly darker and even muddy in low areas. The taste of dry seaweed and burnt rock in the air had been replaced by a softer sensation of dampness, of freshwater and mold and decaying vegetation. The temperature had also dropped. Unfortunately, the horseflies seemed just as comfortable here as farther down.

"¡Agua, agua acá!"

I turned and looked at Rojas. "He says he's found water, sir."

"Where?"

"Back where he is."

That was all it took for me to start running back down the trail, only a few paces behind my interpreter. We found the gunboat skipper kneeling beside a small, moss-covered, water-filled stone pool about ten feet off to one side of the trail. Following the Ecuadoreans' example I knelt next to the pool and tentatively scooped up a handful of water. It was the best I'd ever tasted in my life. Cool, clear, and crisp. After drinking to excess we paused, then wiped off our faces. My two companions turned and looked at me. I looked up and managed to find the sun among the ever-thickening greenery. "We'll continue for another hour and then return."

They looked at each other and shrugged. A good drink of water can be a wonderful thing.

The climb became more challenging as the afternoon advanced, although it was far from truly difficult. At the same time, the vegetation not only thickened but also changed. Trees that resembled oaks or maples began to replace the big-leafed tropical species through which we'd been passing.

About halfway to my self-imposed cutoff time, the ground leveled. A few minutes later I stepped out of the forest into a large, lush valley. A gentle breeze, smelling of forest and damp soil, and oranges, cooled me. Set in the middle of the grassy expanse was one of the farms the skipper had mentioned. And what a farm it was!

In the center was a small but seemingly well-built and comfortable-looking farmhouse with a roofed porch, a barn, and a pen occupied by a dozen cows. Surrounding this were maybe twenty acres of planted land and dozens of fruit trees—not only the bananas, oranges, lemons, and mangos that one might expect but also pears, peaches, and apples.

For many years, Alf, Lisl, and I—and sometimes Erin—had taken Sunday drives up the new parkways north along the Hudson River. We glided past the planted fields and orchards, smelled the air, and stopped at the stands along the roadside to eat fresh fruits and buy fresh vegetables. It had, for me, been a total joy, a release from the grinding pressure, the sense of constriction, of the city. But the vision of this farm and its little valley, only a few miles south of the equator on an island of acrid volcanic ash and lava, was a revelation. It was a fantasy right out of a storybook.

I advanced, Rojas and the petty officer only a few feet behind me, praying there wasn't a shotgun waiting for me. I heard the chickens clucking, rooting around the house, before I saw them. A large black dog shot out from around the side of the house, barking furiously and baring its teeth. "Hello?" I shouted. For some reason that seemed enough to satisfy the dog. It trotted off to one side of the yard and sat, watching us. "Hello?" I tried again. Then I glanced at my companions. The wonder on their faces was obvious.

After shouting once more and not receiving a face full of shot in reply, I stepped up on the porch and knocked politely on the door. Following a second knock I decided nobody was home. I looked around again. All seemed in such perfect order. And so peaceful. I really had no business entering. The last time I'd charged into an unoccupied house on Floreana I'd found a room filled with blood and evil. I clutched the revolver in my right hand and unlatched the unlocked door with my left. The dog watched me carefully but said nothing.

8

The interior of the farmhouse—a modest combined living and dining hall, a small bedroom, a kitchen, and what was either a very large closet or a small storeroom—was sparsely furnished with what must have been homemade furniture. It was immaculately clean, and totally free of blood or dead bodies. Despite the roughness of the furniture it was clear that somebody had worked hard to turn this place into a home. A colorful green spread covered the bed, a white cloth was on the dining table, and embroidered cushions cozied up the chairs. Half a dozen vases and pots filled with colorful and fragrant flowers were placed here and there. Along one wall was a surprisingly large bookcase. I examined the spines of its contents. Most were in some language that looked vaguely German. A few were in English. Almost all appeared to be religious in nature, a conclusion supported by the prints illustrating the life of Christ that shared the walls with various photographs of somebody's family, the people warmly dressed against the northern winter.

We returned to the porch, and I stepped out from under the roof. The sun was at most an hour from the horizon.

"OK," I said, "we have to hurry to get back to the beach before dark."

My companions looked at each other. "Sir," said Rojas, "there's water in the kitchen. Can we get some?"

"Good idea; let's fill up and get going."

The trip back to the beach was understandably faster than the trip up to the farm, but even so it was almost dark when we finally reached the boat. The crew, whom we'd left lounging on the sand, were now pacing up and down, looking nervous. We pulled out to the gunboat, where I had the skipper radio Wreck Bay to report the new murders and that I intended to stay at Floreana one more day to find the owners of the farm and to visit the settlement on the other side of the island. The radio operator at naval headquarters took the message, and I felt a sense of relief. This way there could be no arguments with López. At least not until we got back. I ate aboard the gunboat—rice, beans, some fish the crew had caught during the day, and more plantains—and rowed myself back to *Pegasus* for what I hoped would be a quiet night.

The night did prove quiet. There were no car horns and no squealing of steel on steel as elevated trains passed overhead. And no shotgun blasts ashore or afloat. A gentle breeze blew from the northwest while a long, slow swell from the west barely made it into the bay. Overhead, the sky was a glittering symphony of silver and black. I'd hoped to take advantage of the calm to review what I knew about the murders, but I didn't know much, so my mind wandered off to other matters. I was a good cop, I tried to reassure myself, despite my current predicament. I'd badgered Alf to lean on one of his German American politician friends to get me on the force because I'd believed what the teachers said in school about America being all about justice and decency. I'd wanted to help and protect people. A lot of others had joined just because they needed a job—and at that time there weren't many jobs around. Fortunately, I'd never actually come out and said how I felt at the station house. If I had, I'd have been laughed out into the street.

The next morning the weather was cool and clear, except for the mist wrapped around the highlands. When we landed on the beach this time, we were better prepared; my two companions and I set out equipped with several water bottles and some bread and cheese.

We made good time through the forest, meeting nothing more intimidating than a couple wild goats and only stopping once or twice to catch our breath. We paused at the edge of the grassy plain when I heard a faint noise that sounded human. Once clear of the surrounding trees and undergrowth, the faint noise resolved itself into a voice singing in Spanish. As we approached the farmhouse I spotted a woman positioning a small log for splitting. We turned toward her, and the black dog that had been sitting on the ground beside her jumped to its feet, barking furiously. The woman turned and grabbed the ax lying on the ground next to her, an expression of surprise on her face. She was a very pretty young Ecuadorean. After a moment she leaned down and said something to the dog. The beast barked twice more, then stood silently waiting, I'm sure, for some justification to do something more dramatic.

We stopped about twenty feet away from her. Rojas stepped forward and introduced us. Still holding the ax, she studied us a moment, smiled very slightly, then replied.

"She says 'welcome,' sir, and we must speak with her husband. She doesn't speak English."

Almost before the words were out of Rojas's mouth a tall, blond fellow appeared out of the forest behind us and limped rapidly over. We must have walked right by him without my noticing, I thought a little uneasily. At least he didn't have a shotgun under his arm. He spoke quickly to Rojas in Spanish then turned to me. "I'm Olaf Hanson, and this is my wife, Paquita," he said in English. "You're American?"

"Yes, Frederick Freiman."

"You look German." A look of distaste passed over his face.

"I'm an American, Mr. Hanson."

"Very good. I'm Norwegian. Welcome to my farm, Mr. Freiman. This sailor says you're investigating the murder of the baroness and her two lovers."

"Yes. Did you know about them?"

"Not until he just told us. What happened? Did they all strangle each other? Or maybe shoot?"

"The woman was killed with an ax, and the two men were shot the next night."

Hanson glanced briefly at the ax in his wife's hands. "Do you have any idea who did it and why?" He appeared far more curious than sad.

I told him what I knew. As I did, I noticed that Paquita was concentrating on every word I said. She might not speak English, but it was very possible that she could understand bits and pieces. By the time I was halfway through my account she was pouting, looking accusingly at her husband.

The dog continued to stand beside Paquita, its tongue hanging out, its face exhibiting that inscrutable expression of eager anticipation that dogs so often wear.

"Why are you, an American, investigating this matter?"

"It's a complicated story, but to make it short, I have to find the murderer or Sergeant López will send me to the mainland to be tried for it myself."

"That still doesn't make sense," said Hanson, a look of suspicion on his long, coarse-featured face.

"He thinks I'll understand how the foreign settlers think better than he does."

"Do you speak German?"

"Yes."

"Sergeant López is a very clever fellow. Very dangerous. Watch out for him."

"So I'm learning. Did you know the baroness?" This time I knew Paquita understood my question by the bitter resentment that flushed her face. The ax remained in her hand.

"How could we not? She and her lapdogs arrived several years ago, and she tried to make us all her subjects. She had an unlimited supply of money, so she hired just about everybody on Floreana to build her castle. And from other islands, too. And she said we had to treat her like a baroness. At first she even tried to force her workers to bow to her."

"Did you work for her?"

"No, of course not. Only the Ecuadoreans."

"You seem to be her closest neighbor. How often did you see her?"

"I sold her meat and fruit. Every week or so one of her lapdogs, sometimes her Ecuadorean cook, came to get them."

"She never came?"

"At first, once or twice. After that, no."

"And you never visited her castle?" Anger flashed across Paquita's face.

"No, not if I could avoid it," shouted Olaf. He grabbed the ax from Paquita and slammed the blade into a log. "Once or twice. On business."

"What sort of a businessperson was she?"

"She was a hard negotiator. She could be fierce."

"Do you owe her any money?"

"No. And she owed me none, either."

"You said she had an Ecuadorean cook. The only Ecuadorean I saw there was Sofía, the maid."

"She had four or five servants around the house."

"Where do they live?"

"Some at the settlement at Blackwater Bay; others have little farms spread through the hills."

"What do you know about her past?"

"Nothing. She said she was a baroness and came from Germany. She has—had—a lot of money. She was a very cruel woman, one of the devil's generals. God has taken His revenge on her, and the Earth is now cleaner." As he spoke, Olaf Hanson's eyes flared.

"What about Dr. Ritter and Ernst?"

"They came with her. They lived for her cruelty."

"Did you see either of them the past day or two?"

"No. Not for four or five days." Hanson was pacing back and forth now, clearly agitated.

"Where were you yesterday? We stopped by, and you weren't here."

"At Blackwater Bay with Paquita. Visiting my brother, Piers. You should talk to the Germans."

"Which Germans?"

"The ones on San Cristóbal and Santa Cruz."

"What will they tell me?"

"You talk to them. Now leave me. Tell López that I've helped you as much as I can."

I sighed. This conversation was going nowhere. "Do you know a German named Martin Becker?"

Olaf, who'd already turned away, spun back. "Him! He's different. There's something wrong about him. He's even more evil than the other Germans. He thinks he is a god. He belongs back in Europe, not here."

"Besides thinking he's a god, why else is he so different?"

"He hasn't settled down. He wanders all over asking questions and studying the land and the rocks and asking who owns this and who owns that. He says he's a businessman looking for investments for rich people in Europe. Maybe he is, but something's wrong. I've seen him many times standing on the top of the mountain with his binoculars looking all around as if he's looking for something in particular. Now go!"

"Thank you, Mr. Hanson. Is there a trail that goes to Blackwater Bay?"

"Yes, over there." He pointed.

I glanced at Rojas, who was staring at the fruit trees. "Mr. Hanson, may I buy some fruit from you for me and my companions? We have a long walk ahead of us."

"Take it, take what you want. Get water over there if you need some. Then go."

9

It took us an hour to descend through the temperate forest and the dry, faintly spicy coastal forest to Blackwater Bay, where the air was filled with the sharp perfume of sun-baked, long-dead seafood. The settlement was far smaller than Wreck Bay. There were a dozen wooden houses of various sizes and conditions, two short, narrow piers, and half a dozen fishing boats pulled up on the beach. Beside some of the boats were piles of fish traps and half barrels filled with long lines with hooks every few feet, several being overhauled by their owners, none of whom looked Norwegian. "Ask one of these fishermen if they know where Piers Hanson is," I directed Rojas.

Rojas asked, and the fisherman pointed over my shoulder. "He's in his house, sir. Over there," reported my translator.

I turned. Directly behind me about a hundred feet away and set off by itself was one house that was larger, neater, and better maintained than the others. "Let's go see what Olaf's brother has to say about things," I thought aloud as I led the way up the beach.

After climbing up onto the front porch I knocked on the door, which opened immediately. Piers Hanson looked so much like his brother that they could almost have been twins. I introduced myself and explained my mission. Hanson looked past me a moment, out over the bay, and then invited me in. I turned to Rojas. "I want you and the skipper to wander around the settlement and see what people have to say about the baroness and what they might know about her death. I especially want you to find anybody who worked for her. They must know something."

Rojas nodded and explained the mission to the petty officer, who shot me another of his resentful looks. I could understand how he might feel—he was supposed to be commanding a gunboat, not running errands for me—but we both knew that he would do it or take his chances with Sergeant López, the governor's coldly jovial enforcer.

Hanson told me to take a seat in his living room and disappeared into the kitchen. A moment later he returned with two cool glasses of a juice that tasted like orange but more spicy. "So," he said, settling onto a couch upholstered in a tired floral print, "somebody killed the baroness and her toadies, and López has you doing his work for him. What does he have on you?"

"If I don't find the real killer then I stand trial for it."

"He's a vicious bastard."

"You're a fisherman?"

"Yes, my younger brother is the farmer and I'm the fisherman."

"How well did you know the baroness?"

"I sold fish to her. Usually to her cook or one of those German fools who worshipped her, but I did see her at times. Everybody on Floreana saw her from time to time. The cook lives right here at Blackwater. His name is Elías."

"Did you talk with her?"

"From time to time. She wasn't the absolute bitch that some of these people believe she was."

"Any business disputes?"

"None. We understood each other perfectly."

"How about Ritter and Ernst?" As I asked I looked around the living room. It had a barren air. A dining table in one corner, four or five plain wooden chairs, and a few prints of what must have been Norway. But no books and no other decoration. It didn't look as if Piers was much interested in the homey look.

"Every now and then. Mostly about fish and the weather. They were both very distant and unpleasant fellows. They believed they were very superior. She often acted that way, too."

"Did they ever say anything about the baroness?"

"Only that the rest of us didn't appreciate her as much as she deserved. They were very secretive."

"Did they ever quarrel?"

"I never saw them. What they did in private I can only guess."

As he spoke, Piers glanced out the window, then jumped up and ran across the room, grabbing a rock from a small pile next to the door. He threw the door open, stepped out on the porch, and hurled the rock. A high-pitched cry of pain quickly followed. Hanson slammed the door shut and turned back toward me, a smile of triumph on his face. "I got the little son of a bitch!"

My lack of understanding must have been obvious, for he continued, "The little Ecuadorean brats play around the boats. I've told them not to play around mine, but they've not obeyed. Now maybe they will. Or that little rodent will, anyway."

I thought about all the kids I'd shouted at over the years for playing in the wrong places. Most had been innocent, mindless little fools. A few had been criminals in training. I'd never found it necessary to throw a rock at any of them, or even cuff their ears, although, to be honest, I have roughed up a few teenaged punks from time to time. But they weren't little kids, and they were doing more than just playing in the wrong place.

"Tell me, Mr. Freiman, what do the Americans think about Hitler? Do you think they'll turn against him or accept him as an ally against the Reds?"

My spirits slumped. This conversation wasn't going any better than the one with Olaf. Most of what I knew about Hitler came from the newspapers, which said he was building a new nation and hurting people in the process. On the streets, some said we had to fight, others said we had to concentrate on defending our homeland, and a few said the Nazis were the future. Most of the talk, however, had been about finding work and wondering how the Yankees might do during the coming season. I told Hanson that I really didn't know the answer.

I looked around the room again, comparing it to his brother's house. "Do you have a wife?" The change of subject didn't seem to bother him, although the topic did.

"Yes, Christina. I suppose she's still my wife." His face and the tone of his voice suddenly reeked of anger and resentment. "She didn't like it here, so she went home to Norway."

"When?"

"About two months ago."

I looked again at the couch and suspected that Christina had tried to make a home here but Piers's fury had proven too much for her.

It was time for the second half of my mission. "Do you know a German named Martin Becker?"

"Yes, of course. Everybody does."

"Olaf seems to think he's looking for something."

"Undoubtedly. Everybody who comes to these islands is looking for something."

"Olaf seems to think he's evil in some way."

"Olaf does have an imagination. Becker is strange but not evil. He's a young fellow and can be very interesting and even pleasant in a stiff way."

I sat up. Could this possibly be leading somewhere? "What do you think he's looking for?"

"He's never said, but I can guess."

"Yes?"

"Pirate treasure. For hundreds of years pirates used to hide here and repair their ships. If you believe the stories, there are at least twenty treasures buried on the different islands."

"Do you believe the stories?"

"No, but he's young and probably does."

"Have you seen him recently?"

"No. I heard he got another fisherman to take him to Santa Cruz, or possibly all the way to San Salvador."

"When?"

"A week or two ago. Maybe last week. I don't remember. It's not important."

Becker really did get around, I thought. I'd seen him at Wreck Bay two days ago.

"Do you know which fisherman?"

"Pepe Hernández, I think. He doesn't live here, but he drops by sometimes. He sets some traps a mile or two up the coast."

I nodded.

"Listen to me, Kraut. If you really want to know about the baroness, you go talk to the Herzog brothers at Navy Bay. They're fishermen like me. They get all around these islands."

"Where's Navy Bay?"

"On Santa Cruz." Was there a hint of contempt in his voice at my ignorance? Then it hit me—Santa Cruz, Ana's island.

I finished the juice, thanked Piers Hanson, and started to leave. As I stepped through the door, one final question came to mind. "Why aren't you out fishing today? The weather's fair."

"The weather's usually fair. We fish when we feel like fishing. That's how we do things here.

"I should warn you about Becker," he added as I was half-way across his porch. "He's a smart fellow, but he has one hell of a temper and doesn't like answering questions."

"Thanks for the warning," I said, adding to myself, who does like answering questions around here? Or anyplace else?

I walked rapidly across the rocky sand, my canvas shoes doing nothing to protect my already bruised feet, to the cluster of little wooden shacks that constituted the rest of the settlement. I found Rojas and the petty officer talking to a young, well-built Ecuadorean man. Rojas turned to me. "This is Elías, sir. He was the baroness's cook."

I nodded to Elías and smiled. He struck me as exceptionally well scrubbed, better than me to be honest, his undershirt spotless. Must be the baroness's influence, I thought. "What has he told you?" I asked Rojas.

"He worked for her for about a year. The money was good."

"Ask him how she treated him. Did he get along with her?"

"He did what he was told and got along all right. He says once or twice she said she wanted to sleep with him, but he always refused. He didn't want to get too involved."

"Involved in what?" I asked, assuming the Ecuadorean was fantasizing. Somehow, I couldn't imagine the baroness sleeping with the help.

"In her business. In her life. With the other two Germans. He just wanted to do his job and get paid."

"Did he ever get angry with her?"

"He just did his job."

"Were any of the other Ecuadoreans angry enough to kill her?"

"They just did their jobs and got along."

"What about Dr. Ritter and Ernst? Did he ever see them angry at her or her at them?"

"That was part of the game they played."

"Does he have any idea who might have killed her?"

"Except for her two friends, nobody liked her. She was an outsider. Just like the other Germans. It could have been anybody."

"When was he last at the castle?"

"The day before she was killed, sir. He says he hasn't been back since."

"Does he know where Dr. Ritter and Ernst were when she was killed?"

"No, sir. The last he saw them was when he was last at the castle."

"Who else was there?"

"Nobody, sir, except Sofía, the maid."

"Did the baroness have any visitors during the week or so before she was killed?"

Elías paused a moment to think, then replied.

"He says he can only remember one visitor, several days before she was killed. It was Mr. Thompson."

"Who's he?"

"He's an American with a big sailboat," explained Rojas. "He's visiting on vacation. For adventure."

"Did they argue?"

"No, just the opposite. They were very friendly."

"Were Ritter and Ernst upset about that?"

"He says he has no way of knowing. May he go now?" Rojas was really getting into the translation bit. Not only was he reporting the words, but his tone of voice reproduced the emotions that were so clear on the cook's face.

I checked my watch and looked up at the sun. "Thank him. We should eat and get going."

"Yes, sir."

We found a waist-high rock under a stunted tree and settled down to enjoy our lunch of rice, beans, and plantain slices. There was something about Elías that didn't ring true. He had trouble looking me in the eye, and he had a number of small bruises and welts on his arms and shoulders. Cooks who got along with their employers didn't end up with bruises. Burns, maybe, or cuts, but not bruises like those. Unless he was a brawler of some sort, a guy who just couldn't keep out of fights. And I didn't know what to make of his claim that the baroness wanted to sleep with him. It was possible, I suppose, but the woman seemed to have a great many more impressive choices. Somebody had once told me that all men who speak Spanish have a thing about being real men. In fact, I thought, that applied as well to the guy who had said it. Maybe the cook was just embellishing his manhood.

What have I learned today? I asked myself. That the baroness had been one hell of a woman, even if she'd also been a bitch. Based on Paquita's reactions, and much that was left unsaid, the baroness had managed to seduce both Norwegians, possibly Elías, and some American yachtsman named Thompson.

How Ritter and Ernst felt about this remained unclear. She'd made enemies by trying to lord it over everybody. As things now stood, just about every man and woman in Las Encantadas could reasonably be considered a suspect. I knew a great deal more than I had twenty-four hours before and still I knew nothing. The means were as obvious as the motives, but the particulars remained totally unknown.

We were back at the castle by three in the afternoon. I opened the doors and took another look at Ritter and Ernst. So far nothing had nibbled on them, although it was still hot in the room and they were beginning to both bloat and reek. I considered moving them someplace, but where? Or at least wrapping them in sheets or blankets. No reason to, I decided. López might want to see them as they lay. I stepped out onto the patio again, closed the doors, and looked out at *Pegasus*, anchored in the still water. The breeze had died, leaving only the long, slow swell. There was no way I could sail back to Wreck Bay without a breath of wind. "Rojas, tell the skipper that we're going to tow my boat back to San Cristóbal. You ride with me."

"Yes, sir." I think the kid was getting to like his new job. Hiking and riding around with me had to be more interesting than scrubbing, painting, and walking around with a rifle, or whatever else it was that he would be doing at Wreck Bay.

The tow was long, slow, and uneventful. As I steered to stay in the gunboat's wake, I went over the events of the last two days. Ana was right. Somebody knew about the baroness, and about Ritter and Ernst, and I was now willing to bet there was more than one somebody. Undoubtedly on Floreana, and very possibly on some of the other islands. They were, after all, only a few hours' sail apart. Less in a motorboat. Everybody I'd spoken to had plenty to say about the baroness, and about their neighbors. But, at best, all I'd uncovered were hints, many of which contradicted each other. How many people really knew who'd committed the murders, and how many just suspected one of their neighbors? How many were trying to disappear into the woodwork, to protect themselves or somebody else, and how many were trying to pin it on somebody? And how many believed it was a matter of good riddance to bad garbage and didn't care who'd done the deed?

When we finally reached Wreck Bay, the only visible lights ashore were two windows in naval headquarters and one dim white light at the end of the pier. After *Pegasus* was securely anchored, I thanked Rojas and told him to go ashore with the rest of the gunboat crew. I then grabbed a lukewarm beer and settled back in the cockpit, looking up at the stars.

Prior to taking up sailing with Alf, I'd never paid much attention to the night sky, probably because it's almost impossible to see in Manhattan. But once you're at sea, and the night is clear and quiet, the stars are brilliant, overwhelming. If you let them, they fill your mind and soul and then absorb you. You dive into them and find yourself in some distant time and place, far from the petty concerns of life and death. In my case they also clear my mind and help me to think and see through impassible thickets.

I sipped the beer and allowed myself to float up toward the scintillating mass of silver-blue light. Relaxing, I wondered idly how I was going to solve this mess and save my own hide. I tried to focus on the baroness's mangled body, but the celestial spheres wouldn't let me. All I could see was the face of Ana de Guzmán, winking at me. I found myself smiling foolishly. Was she pretty, I asked myself. Yes, but not really what you would call cute. She was compelling. I could think of no other word. I knew so little about her, yet I found myself aching for her. It was her spirit, I thought. Even the little I'd had the chance to experience. She seemed her own woman but not one totally focused on herself. She was a mix of the regal and the practical. I had no trouble imagining her crawling into a huge machine to oil the gears. At the same time, I could also imagine her in my arms, dancing.

I snorted at my own foolishness and sat up. Why was I even thinking about her? She was a South American aristocrat, without doubt sickeningly wealthy, and I knew damn well that her type of people were even more stuck-up than the Astors or the Mellons. While she was at Barnard College I was slogging through the streets and alleys of Hell's Kitchen. Erin was my kind of girl. Erin had spirit too, even if she didn't have buckets of money. Spirit that Sergeant McGrath was undoubtedly beating out of her at this very minute. Erin was as lost to me now as if they were singing her requiem. I stood a moment, feeling deflated and very lonely. Was I betraying Erin as thoroughly as I had betrayed Alf by stealing his boat?

Yes, I admitted to myself.

I started to throw the empty beer bottle over the side, then remembered that bottles, like most manufactured goods, were very valuable in the islands and I'd promised to return the empties. I'd had a long day and found no answers. It was time for me to dive into my bunk for a well-earned rest. Before I'd even managed to position my pillow, however, I heard a boat come alongside and felt a bump. A moment later a dark shape appeared in the companionway, obliterating the blue-white beauty of the stars. "Fritz, welcome home. I hear you've been a very busy fellow. You must tell me all about it."

10

I was bone tired, and thinking about Erin and Alf had depressed me If I'd been a free man I'd have told the sergeant to go to hell, but I wasn't free, and my depression hadn't quite reached the point of suicide, so all I said was "Yes, I've been damn busy, and so has our murderer."

"Tell me!" He sounded rather tired himself.

"Somebody blew Ritter and Ernst to hell with a shotgun. Made a real mess of them. Four empty shells, so I assume between them they were shot four times. I couldn't find Ritter's gun, so maybe that was the murder weapon. The killer must have taken it with him." López was sitting in the companionway, his feet on the stairs and his body continuing to block the starlight, so I was speaking into a near-absolute darkness. "I questioned half the people who live on Floreana—everybody I could find who I figured might know something. And was willing to talk to me. I didn't see anything else worth noting at the murder scene except a lacquered box with a broken lock in the baroness's bedroom."

"What was in it?"

"Their passports and some sort of grant for the property." I decided not to mention the photographs, which I had pocketed. "I left it there so you could look over the scene in case I missed anything."

"Are you suggesting that robbery may have been involved?"

"That's possible. The box had been forced open, and there was no money in it; all their animals have disappeared from the barn. But it doesn't feel right. And Seaman Rojas assures me that the neighbors might very well kill the baroness and her subjects but not in order to rob them. He thinks the locals made off with the goods after they knew all three were dead."

"You think Rojas's opinions are worth listening to?" There was a mixture of contempt and curiosity in the voice that came out of the dark.

"He's bright. He knows more about the Galápagos than I do. He's proving useful."

"Very well. I'll arrange for the disposal of the bodies. Who did you question?"

"Hanson. Both Hansons. And Elías, the cook."

"All possible suspects, especially the Norwegians. The younger one is a religious fanatic. He might have decided he was doing God's work. Or maybe it was that wife of his. She may have suspected something of her husband's dalliance. And the other one, the fisherman, he can be violent. I don't know about the cook, but I suppose it's possible. He may have been angry with her. She had a way of upsetting people. You should question them all again."

"Piers Hanson said I should talk to the Herzog brothers, but they don't live on Floreana."

"That means nothing. We're an island people. We all have friends on many islands. And enemies. Question the Herzogs, especially Gregor."

"I'd also like to find Becker again and talk to him. I have a feeling, and I don't know why, that he may be involved. I'm always suspicious of mystery men."

"Becker? Don't worry about him. He was at Wreck Bay. The commandant has become obsessed with him. Your job is to find the murderer."

I knew I shouldn't argue with López—he was reminding me more and more of Sergeant McGrath—so I didn't. "Should I keep using the gunboat to get around? As you say, island life requires a lot of boat rides."

"Yes, unless I say otherwise. And keep Rojas with you. You'll also need money. Here."

As he spoke I heard him moving down the ladder into the cabin. He stopped next to the bunk and handed me a large wad of paper sucres along with a handful of coins. "Is there anything else I should know?"

"As soon as I find out, I'll tell you."

"OK then, Fritz. Good night." His tone was brusque, by no means warm or approving of my efforts.

The boat rocked slightly, there was a muffled bump, and López was gone, but the sense of unease he caused me remained. The sergeant was cold—and not at all above black-mail and extortion—but I knew that most people considered those tactics just part of being a cop. He was, to all appear-ances, competent, dedicated, resourceful, energetic, and not too given to violence. At least I hadn't seen any. I should have been reasonably comfortable working for him—even as a forced laborer—but I wasn't. That was why I hadn't men-tioned my nagging desire to know where Ritter and Ernst had been when the baroness was killed. It's an obvious question but easily overlooked when one assumes the two love slaves—if that's what they really were—couldn't possibly have killed her. And even more so when they themselves were killed the next night. If the question was obvious to me, then it must have been obvious to the sergeant. Yet he hadn't asked it.

I awoke the next day around seven, physically rested but mentally fuzzy. I rummaged around a few minutes in the galley and confirmed that there was no food aboard *Pegasus*. I considered heading for the mess at the naval headquarters but decided to be adventurous. After relieving myself and scrubbing my face and teeth, I turned toward the ladder up into the cockpit and paused next to the chart table. I studied the chart that was unrolled there and located Wreck Bay, on San Cristóbal, and Santa Cruz, Ana's island. Fifty miles apart at most. Just a short commute by Galápagos standards. Ana and her family were going to have a visitor, I assured myself. Soon. Possibly when I visited the Herzogs.

It was going to be another beautiful day. I rowed to the pier and tied the dinghy opposite the gunboat. The unsmiling gunboat skipper watched, his hand tapping the rail. I climbed up on the pier and started for the gunboat, wondering how I was going to communicate, when Rojas popped up out of a hatch. "Good morning, Seaman Rojas," I greeted him, with an internal sigh of relief.

"Good morning, sir."

"Tell the skipper that I'll go eat now and return in an hour. We must get under way then."

Rojas repeated the message, and the petty officer nodded.

"Have you had breakfast?" I asked my translator.

"Yes, sir."

"What was it?"

"Rice and beans, sir. And some fruit."

"Come join me. I want to talk to you."

"As you wish, sir. Where?"

Where? I didn't want to go back to the place López had taken me for a beer. It was too small and depressing. "Suggest something."

"How about the most lively place in town, although not in the morning? And they have good food, too."

"Lead the way."

The hour was early, but the settlement was fully awake and alive. On the beach two fishing boats were being launched while a party of children and women walked slowly along the tide line, looking for something among the half-dried seaweed. At the other end of the beach a marine iguana was doing the same. Smoke curled out of half a dozen chimney pipes, and the almost toothless carpenter was hard at work planing another plank. The air was filled with the smells and sounds of sizzling coconut oil, plantains, and goat, mixed with the sharp smell of the sea and the faint, heavy smell of humanity.

"What do you want to eat, sir?" asked my guide as we walked past the hole-in-the-wall where I'd drunk with my boss.

"Eggs, I guess. And some potatoes and meat." I'd set out to be adventurous, but now I thought I might really want an honest-to-God American breakfast.

"What kind of eggs, sir?"

"What kind are there?"

"Turtle eggs and two or three different kinds of bird eggs."

"Hens' eggs?"

"Yes, sir. The others taste like fish. Pork?"

"Yes. And we can get potatoes, can't we?"

"Yes, sir. Follow me."

I followed Rojas through the narrow passages between the weather-stained buildings. Some were just homes, but many had shops or businesses on the first floor. Despite the rising sun, shadows remained in the corners of the passages, like a sea mist that hadn't quite burned off.

We emerged on the far side of the settlement, a side I hadn't visited yet. Rojas led me into an open-air restaurant that looked out on the rocky shore. Over the gate a sign read RESTAURANTE MIRAMAR. Despite the sandy floor, I concluded this was one of the settlement's tonier eating places—very possibly its only tony one. My guide led me to one of the two empty tables. I looked out at the shore and at the other customers seated at the dozen or so tables, while Rojas ordered breakfast for me. "Coffee, sir?"

"Yes. Is there cows' milk?"

"Of course, sir. Fruit?"

"What do you suggest?"

"I like mango, sir."

"Then get me some mango," I directed, not having the slightest idea what I was ordering. "And what do you want?"

"Nothing, sir, thank you. I've eaten."

"You must have some coffee."

"That's kind of you, sir."

"Did you ever meet the baroness or her two friends?" I asked while we waited for our food.

"No, sir. I saw them once or twice here in Wreck Bay. Everybody has to come here from time to time to deal with the government."

"What did you hear about them?"

"That they weren't popular. That they were strange."

"What about those people we spoke to yesterday? The Hansons?"

"Señora Hanson is very pretty. Her husband is very religious."

"And the other one, the fisherman?"

"I don't have an opinion, sir."

"What about Elías, the cook?"

"I think he'll have to find a new job."

I burst out laughing.

"Sir?"

"I apologize, Rojas."

"You must understand, sir, that I'm a navy sailor, not a Galapaguino. I'm from the mainland. I'll serve here a few years and then go home. I don't totally understand these people, especially the foreigners."

"Where did you learn to speak English?"

"My father works for a British company, and they encourage their employees to learn English, sir."

"How did you end up in the navy?"

"My father didn't want me in the army. He was in the army and now has only one arm."

"Do you have a girlfriend back home?"

"Not really, sir. There are many girls I like, but none is special."

"Here?"

"No, sir."

"Seaman Rojas," I continued, learning forward, "how did all of Wreck Bay learn I was a policeman?"

Rojas stared at me a moment. "Santiago, sir, that old sailor, overheard you talking with Sergeant López. He speaks some English."

"And who do you work for?"

"I'm assigned to help you."

"You work for me, and I work for Sergeant López, is that right?"

The boy—for that was essentially what he was—started to squirm, and I decided that he was basically honest. We both knew that we both worked for López and that we both reported to López. I was reasonably certain Rojas's translations had been accurate—otherwise I would have seen evidence of confusion—but I was now also certain he was required to report everything I saw, heard, and said to the sergeant. Which meant the only thing he wasn't sharing with López was what I might be thinking. Unless he could read minds.

"Rojas," I said with a smile, "I think I now understand you, and I think you now understand me. We understand what we're each expected to do by people more powerful than us. You've already helped me, and I think you'll help me a lot more as time passes. I look forward to working with you."

"Thank you, sir."

By now our food had arrived. I settled back and grabbed my fork as Rojas took a deep draft of coffee and seemed to relax slightly. I tried the yellow mango. Not bad, although it did have a slightly medicinal aftertaste. And it was a little stringy. The pork, eggs, and potatoes were just what I'd hoped for.

I glanced around the restaurant again. Most of the other customers were Ecuadoreans, slightly better dressed than many I'd seen but still far from elegant. They'd studied us briefly as we walked in, then returned to whatever they were discussing. The three men at one table, however, kept looking at us, then talking intently among themselves, then looking again. I knew they weren't locals, and I don't like being stared at, so I glowered at them. One, a tall fellow dressed in worn jeans, an equally worn sport shirt, and gold wire-rimmed glasses, stood and walked over. "Name's Bob," he said, holding out his hand. "You're the American López shanghaied into tracking down whoever killed the crazy German bitch." It wasn't a question, it was a statement.

"Fred Freiman," I replied, standing up and offering my hand. "You seem to know a lot about me, and I know nothing about you, except that you're also American."

"Bob Thompson," he said. "From San Diego. That schooner out there is mine." He pointed out to the harbor at a large schooner that was almost totally hidden by one of the buildings that enclosed the eating area.

Thompson, I thought. According to the cook, this must be the baroness's American friend. "What are you doing in the Galápagos?"

"Sightseeing. This is our third visit to Wreck Bay. We've visited half a dozen of the islands—amazing animal life. Check out the tortoises—they're hundreds of years old. But you have to know where to find them."

Rojas had mentioned the huge tortoises the day before, when we were struggling through the brush on Floreana. "Who's with you?"

"Two other Americans—old friends—and four crew."

"Ever visit Floreana?"

"Twice. Even visited the baroness. The late baroness."

"What do you know about her?"

"That she was probably German and probably a baroness." Thompson paused a second, the aggressive, cynical expression on his face relaxing into a more meditative one. "She was a very lonely woman. She acted tough, and she was, but I think she was also very vulnerable in a way. To be honest, once or twice I thought she was a little bit insane. Sometimes it was as if she wasn't there. As if her body was here but she was someplace else. And sometimes I could feel that she was scared, but I don't know of what."

"Did you ask?"

"Of course not! She would have thrown me out. She didn't want any help."

"What do you know about her past?"

"Nothing, to be honest."

"Do you know why she came to the Galápagos?"

"I think she was looking for some sort of freedom. Freedom to do something or be something, but that's really little more than a guess."

"What about her two friends?"

"Nuts. What else can I say?" All suggestion of meditation vanished as his face hardened again.

"When did you last see the baroness?"

"A week or so ago."

Either Thompson or Elías was lying, and it seemed likely the American had the best reason to do so. I looked at my watch. "How much longer will you be here?"

"At Wreck Bay?"

"And in the islands."

"Wreck Bay another few days. The islands, maybe another week or two."

"What do you do for a living that you can own that big schooner and spend months sightseeing?"

"Family money."

"I'll be back tomorrow, and I'll want to talk some more with you."

"If I'm still here we can have a beer."

"I hope you'll be here."

"I'll be here if it's convenient. I'm not worried about López." Thompson then spun on his heel and returned to his table.

11

Rojas and I made it back to the pier in just over the hour I'd promised the skipper, who was staring at us with a neutral, if long-suffering, expression. The instant I had both feet aboard the vessel, the lines were cast off. We slid out of the harbor into the deep blue waters of the cold Humboldt Current for the fifty-mile voyage to Navy Bay on Santa Cruz. Thanks to a minor problem with the engine, water in one of the fuel tanks, we didn't arrive until midafternoon.

Navy Bay, like all the others I'd seen in Las Encantadas, was round and wide open on one side, strongly suggesting that it had started life as a volcanic crater. Off to the right was a cluster of wooden dwellings much like those at Wreck Bay, only the cluster was smaller, more the size of Blackwater Bay. Off to the left, however, was something more impressive. A line of rocks had been built up a few feet offshore, creating a low seawall. The area behind the seawall had been filled in with rocks and sand, creating a level platform about a hundred feet square. On one side of the platform were three smallish wooden houses. On the other were the beginnings of several stone walls. "The skipper says that's where the Herzog brothers live," reported Rojas, pointing at the construction project. By the time the gunboat had turned into the wind, anchored, and put a rowboat over the side, three Herzogs had gathered to watch our approach. Two men and a woman. Like all the foreign settlers I'd met so far, they were tanned, weathered, and wiry. None of the Europeans seemed to get fat in Las Encantadas.

"What language do they prefer?" I asked Rojas, who repeated the question to the skipper.

"He says German, English, Spanish—it makes no difference to them."

The boat drifted up to the rocky side of the man-made platform. One of the men knelt down and grabbed the gunnel. He was short, slightly bowlegged, so very wiry he was almost springy, and about my age. "Welcome," he said with a smile that stretched from ear to ear. "I'm Gregor Herzog. You must be the American everybody's talking about."

"I am," I replied as I reached for a stone to pull myself out of the boat. "Come along, Rojas," I directed as I stood. "Tell the oarsmen to go back to the gunboat. We'll signal for them when we're ready to leave."

"No, no," said Herzog, "they're hot, tired, and thirsty. Have them tie up to that wooden dock over there and get something to drink while we talk. You're here to talk, aren't you?"

"Yes," I said. "That's very kind of you." I nodded for Rojas to relay the invitation to the sailors.

"This is my wife, Carla," said Gregor, pointing at the lithe, attractive woman standing off to one side with a tall, bearded fellow. Carla had a clever, almost fox-like face with eyes that radiated an intense but guarded passion. And she didn't look German; more Mediterranean, maybe. Something like Ana.

"And that's Kaspar, my brother."

"Fred Freiman."

We all nodded and shook hands. "Seaman Rojas, sir," sputtered my startled translator when Gregor grabbed his hand and shook it.

"It's hot," said Gregor. "Let's get out of the sun and have some lemonade." With that he led the way—practically bouncing with energy as he went—toward one of the three wooden houses. As we walked I glanced at Carla and Kaspar. The bearded brother had a faint, almost amused smile on his face. The wife had a considerably more strained one.

"You have a major construction project here," I remarked, looking around.

"Yes," said Gregor, his pride evident. "We plan to stay for a long time, so we're building in stone. Those walls over there will be our new cistern, to hold the rainwater from when it rains, which isn't that often. As it is, we can catch and save some, but we still have to get water from the springs inland. Once the cistern is done, we build our new houses."

A young, blonde woman walked in the door just after we had entered the house. "Ah, Karen," said Gregor, "meet Fred Freiman, the American who Sergeant López has gotten to do his dirty work for him."

Karen, who turned out to be Kaspar's wife, shook my hand and then followed Carla into the kitchen.

I looked out the window, at the other two wooden houses. "You have another brother?"

"Yes," Gregor assured me, "Albrecht. He's on his way to the mainland, on business."

"When did he leave?"

"On the Guayaquil boat, two days ago."

An alarm went off in my head. "When will he be back?"

Gregor frowned briefly, then burst into laughter. "I think López picked the right man to do his hunting. Yes, Albrecht could have done it and then run away. Except he was right here. Kaspar took him to Wreck Bay the day the ship sailed. He'll be back in a few weeks."

I nodded, thinking I'd have to talk to the sergeant about having the Guayaquil police talk to Gregor's brother. "So, you're glad you came here?"

"Glad! Do you understand what's happening in Germany?" Gregor's smile had returned, then disappeared again. "The German people have lost what little sense they ever had. Before this is over, the whole world will wish it had moved here. Life is hard, but we're free to do pretty much what we want to do." For a moment I thought he was going to jump to his feet and start waving his arms.

"You're fishermen?"

"Yes, except Carla and Karen have a big garden and some pigs and goats. We can't eat only fish."

"Where do you fish?"

"All over. We fish where the fish are."

"Do you ever fish near Floreana?"

The smile reappeared on Gregor's face. "You mean the baroness's island? Yes. I have some lobster traps there. As I said, we fish everywhere."

"There are more than enough fish and lobster around here," snapped Carla as she walked in with a tray of lemonades. "You don't have to go so far all the time."

Gregor continued to smile. "Carla worries about the dangers of the sea; she thinks I may drown. But we got here, didn't we? We sailed all the way from Hamburg."

"Yes," she replied darkly, "the dangers of the sea."

"So tell me, Fred, what have you learned about the baroness's murder?"

"Very little, except that her two friends were also killed, the next day."

"Oh? I hadn't heard about that."

"What do you know about her? And them?"

"The same as everybody else, I'm sure. That she may have been a baroness, that she had a lot of money, and that she liked men."

"Why did she—they—come here?"

"I would say the same reason as all of us. Either she was running from something or looking for a place where she could be herself. I don't think she liked the Nazis, although she sometimes acted like one herself. I wouldn't be surprised if she had an enemy or two of her own back in Germany."

"Did you know her?"

"I sold her some fish and sometimes saw her at Wreck Bay. Once or twice. She was very secretive. But there are many stories about her."

While Gregor discussed the baroness, I noticed that Carla was staring at him with a fixed expression, her lemonade untouched.

"As far as I can tell she wasn't very popular."

"So I think too, but I never saw her do anything really bad. But then I didn't have to share an island with her." Gregor chuckled.

"Kaspar," I asked the bearded brother, who had remained silent as he listened to the exchange, "can you help me here with any information?"

"I know no more about the woman than Gregor does," he replied in between sips of lemonade.

I leaned back and took a sip of my own drink. Once again I'd run up against the same brick wall—nobody liked the baroness, some hated her, and not a soul gave a damn that she was dead, much less wanted to know who'd killed her. Except López. And me—in part because López cared so much and in part because I did.

"Of course you know the Hanson brothers?"

"Of course," agreed Gregor.

"What do you know about them?"

"An interesting situation," said Gregor, settling back in his chair. "Their father is a very severe, no-nonsense preacher back in Norway, which is undoubtedly one reason why they're here. From what they say about him, he considers even taking a deep breath to be a sin that God will punish with total ferocity."

"What about the brothers?"

"The brothers," said Kaspar, "are the father. Each of them is half of the father." I must have looked confused because Kaspar continued, "Olaf is insanely religious—he sees sin everywhere—but whatever his feelings, he never seems to call God's wrath down on those he doesn't like. Piers seems to have forgotten about God but not about wrath and revenge. He can be a very violent fellow."

Yes, he can be, I thought, remembering my visit with him. "Do you know Martin Becker?"

"He's a Nazi, a Fascist," snapped Carla, her eyes flaming.

"We don't know that," said Gregor.

"Yes, we do. I talked to him at Wreck Bay one day. I guess he doesn't talk to the rest of you. Only to women. Or maybe you don't listen."

"Do you know what he's doing here?"

"Making trouble. Bringing all that shit we left in Europe over here."

Gregor leaned over to kiss his wife on the cheek, I suppose to try to calm her down. She swatted him away and walked into the kitchen, her eyes still blazing.

"He's been wandering around the islands for several months now. I don't know why López doesn't know everything there is to know about him. He knows everything about everybody else. I've never seen Becker do anything bad."

"You've seen him a lot?"

"Seen him, not talked to him, except to say hello. He keeps popping up everywhere, just like those Americans in their big schooner. Whenever I go someplace to check my traps they're either just leaving when I arrive or just arriving when I leave."

"Even at Floreana?"

"Yes."

"Which?"

"Both. At different times."

"You all came here to escape the Nazis?" I asked.

"We came here because we couldn't breathe in Germany," snapped Gregor. "There was no food, no money, and no hope. The Depression may be all over the world, but it's especially bad there, although some say it's better now, since we left. The Kaiser destroyed the country in the war, and then the victors—yes, you Americans and the British and French—ground our faces in it and totally bankrupted us. The people were angry and hungry and terrified and stupid. It was all a great mound of garbage, and the Nazis just grew out of the slime."

"And it was a great adventure," added Carla, bursting out of the kitchen, her eyes warning her husband not to cut her off. "How excited we were when we sailed out of Hamburg

on that old sailboat. Gregor had told me this place would
be almost like Italy. And how scared I was. I was so happy to
be leaving the snow and sleet, and at the same time so certain
that we would all die long before we saw the sun again. The
wind, the waves, the darkness. But we made it, although
the boat did sink about a year after we arrived."

"You came over in a sailboat?"

"Yes, just like you. Gregor, Kaspar, Albrecht, and me.
Karen was already here; her family lives on San Cristóbal."

"And you like it here?"

"We certainly don't plan to move," said Gregor.

I took another sip of lemonade and digested what they
were telling me, not that it seemed related to the murders.

"It's Saturday, you know," announced Carla suddenly. "You
have a girlfriend back home? A wife?"

I thought of Erin, and my pain must have shown.

"It's like that, eh?" asked Carla. "Well, you're a good-
looking fellow, and you don't seem too stupid. We may have
a friend for you. Right, Gregor?"

Gregor chuckled.

"We all work hard here, so we have good parties on Saturday nights with a few guests. You stay the night. Rojas,
too. We may have a friend for him if the Echeverrías bring
their girl. Tell the navy to go back to Wreck Bay and come
get you tomorrow. It's Saturday night there, too, and many
of the sailors have families. Or friends."

I looked at Gregor, who was nodding encouragingly, as
were Kaspar and Karen.

"Don't worry," urged Carla, "we have plenty of food and
beer and our own wine. We can eat, drink, sing, and dance.
On second thought, better tell the navy to come get you
Monday."

Rojas was nodding along with everybody else. I was totally outvoted.

"Do you know the de Guzmáns?" I asked. "They live somewhere on this island."

"Yes. They're very nice people," replied Carla. "Do you know them?"

"I've met Ana a few times. I was thinking about visiting them while I'm here."

"There's no time to visit them tonight. You should give them some warning. That's only polite."

Several hours later, the lowering sun had painted a golden path across the dark-blue waters of Navy Bay, and I was slumped in a chair under one of the scrawny, thirsty trees that so favor the Galápagos shore. About twenty feet away a pair of marine iguanas were catching the late rays as they searched listlessly through the long, fingerlike roots of the mangroves. Out in the bay a small pod of porpoises was rummaging around for dinner while a fishing boat sailed slowly toward the other settlement. A bird rustled in the tree above me. Rojas was stretched out in Gregor's living room while the Herzogs were all comfortable in their own beds. We were all resting, waiting for the party.

After I sent the gunboat back to Wreck Bay, Gregor and Kaspar had insisted on giving me and my aide a full tour. We started, understandably, with their fishing boats, which they'd been caulking with strands of pitch-soaked Manila rope shortly before we arrived. Each was about thirty feet long and, to my eye, well built and fastidiously maintained, in contrast to the unpainted, crudely built boats on the beach at Wreck Bay. Even their little auxiliary engines, one-cylinder diesels, were just short of polished. You can take the German out of Germany, I thought, but you can't take Germany out of the

German. Then they'd shown me their fish traps and paced out the extent of every wall of every structure they planned to build on the platform. We continued on, without a pause, to admire their goats, pigs, chickens, and vegetable garden. Carla and Karen, having finished with the basic preparations for the party, joined us near the end of the tour, and we all had another beer before retiring for a short nap to restore our energy.

They'd all managed to fall asleep almost immediately, but I hadn't even tried. I had some serious thinking to do. I was worried, confused, and scared. I was now certain that if I continued investigating in this way, I'd never find the murderer—or murderers. If I didn't solve the murders, how serious was López about shipping me off to some man-made hell on the mainland?

As the sun edged closer to the horizon, the wind began to pick up. I watched the ripples bulk up and start to tumble over those ahead of them, and a nagging suspicion forced its way to the forefront of my thoughts. It had been there for a while, but I'd been so busy acting out chapter 1 in the detective manual that I'd brushed it aside. López didn't expect me to solve the murders! He didn't even want me to. He wanted a somebody, a believable somebody, to send to the mainland to be tried for the crimes. But it couldn't be any somebody; it couldn't be the wrong somebody.

Whatever was happening around me in these shadowy, elusive islands, with a mad governor and clans of out-of-place Germans, was much bigger than just a few murders. A war was coming. A mysterious German and a brash, aggressive American yachtsman were drifting around up to who knew what. Both were acting as if they owned the place. And then there was López himself. He was a player, too. I was going

12

I sat up with a snap and watched intently, all thoughts of the baroness, Becker, Thompson, even López blowing away in the breeze, as the launch turned into the bay. I rubbed my forehead and wished I hadn't let Gregor and Carla feed me so many beers. Between the powerful equatorial sun and the alcohol I felt logy, washed out. I had to keep my wits about me if I was ever to leave Las Encantadas. More important, I desperately wanted to be awake and alert for the party. Ana might enjoy playing silly games from time to time, but I was certain she had no interest in beer-addled fools. She'd made it clear she'd outgrown them in New York.

The launch's arrival was no surprise. Earlier, before disappearing for her nap, Carla had let the cat out of the bag by telling me the real reason I didn't have to visit the de Guzmáns. Ana was coming to the party. When she'd told me I'd smiled.

"How well do you know her, Fred?"

"I just met her for a few minutes. She seemed very forthright."

"And she's also very pretty. No?"

"Yes."

"And fun. She's one of the few people around here who knows something about the world. She and her parents have been our friends almost since we first arrived. They won't be coming tonight, but they have in the past."

"Do they have a car?"

"Yes, but there's no road between here and there, so they use their launch."

I watched the launch approach and felt that pleasant tingling from head to foot. My worries about López and the bastards back in Manhattan blew away with the late afternoon breeze. She *was* very pretty and also a little . . . not really tough, but she knew her mind.

I was the only person standing on the little dock as the launch came alongside. Ana, standing next to Roberto, was dressed more or less as before, in dungarees with a long-sleeved cotton shirt and some sort of halter underneath.

"Ah, Mr. Freiman," she said, showing only the faintest evidence of surprise. "I hope your boss isn't here too."

My eyes fell to the dock, along with my heart. Had she classified me as nothing more than López's flunky, as some sort of cur in service to a yet greater one?

She studied my expression a moment, then smiled again. "I'm sorry, I've done it again, haven't I? Let me start over. Ah, Mr. Freiman, what a great pleasure it is to see you here. What a great surprise. Carla has outdone herself."

My heart started beating again as I took the launch's lines and secured them to the dock. I straightened up and looked at Ana.

"Of course he's not here," she continued, "not among civilized people. The *sargento* is a vile spider who spins webs of steel and traps the innocent in them. And when I saw you in Wreck Bay you didn't look happy to be one of those he's trapped."

"No, I'm not."

She held out a small, white canvas seabag. I took it, and she jumped over onto the dock, then said something in Spanish to Roberto. Her launch captain and bodyguard nodded and smiled as he shut down the diesel engine. Damn it, I thought, I'm going to have to concentrate on learning Spanish. It was bad enough being "the Dutchman" in New York, isolated and ignored. It was proving intolerable here.

When we reached the houses, all remained as quiet as it had been before. Not even the finches were screeching. Ana stood a moment, deep in thought, then looked at the now-vanishing sun. "Is this where the party is?" she demanded in a loud voice. Then, with a mischievous smile, she started pounding on the door to Carla and Gregor's house. "The Echeverrías will be here any minute."

"Ana," shouted Carla from inside. The door flew open, and the hostess appeared with her husband following. "Welcome, welcome. Put your bag inside and let's get started."

The last guests, Héctor and Luz Echeverría, arrived with a basket of fruit from their farm a mile or so inland and a sixteen-year-old daughter named Alicia, who brought a twinkle to Rojas's eyes. By now, Roberto had demolished a beer and headed off to spend the night with friends on the other side of the bay.

We settled around a sort of picnic table set in the middle of the platform. "Have you learned anything about who did those terrible murders?" asked Luz Echeverría. Since she spoke no English, Rojas was translating.

"No," I admitted, "and I'm beginning to wonder if anybody cares."

"I doubt anybody cares about the woman and the two men, unless they owed money to somebody, but we don't like that sort of thing happening. It makes us worry."

I'd been wrong, I thought. Not because anybody cared about the victims but because the killing itself upset the islanders. The sane ones, anyway. "I wish I knew more," I answered lamely. "I really wish I did."

"Anyway," added Héctor Echeverría almost cheerfully, "these murders may be the least of our problems. If the generals manage to overthrow the president we'll see big changes, even out here. And if the generals prove to be as incompetent as they have in the past, we'll all end up citizens of Peru, not that their generals are any smarter."

"What about the war in Europe?" asked Luz. "You all know so much more about such things than we do."

"I think that depends on what the United States does," offered Kaspar. "What do you think, Fred?"

I wanted to say that I was just a dumb New York cop, but I didn't. I'd made it through high school—in fact I was one of the few in my graduating class who had the faintest idea where Ecuador was—but I knew very little about politics. Not even station house politics, as it had turned out. "I think we'll get involved, just like the last war. President Roosevelt hates Hitler."

"But what about the people?" continued Luz. "You're German, aren't you? Aren't many Americans German?"

I had to think a moment to explain something I'd never tried to explain before. "There are some American Nazi groups, and they're damned noisy, but most German Americans are in America because they, or their parents or grandparents, didn't want to be in Germany. Like the Herzogs. As for the rest, it's all very far away. They don't want to get involved. They've got enough problems right at home."

Despite the wind, the night was warm, and we'd all had more than a few beers. "Like *some* of the Herzogs," grumbled Kaspar in a loud voice.

Gregor spun and looked at him intently, almost threateningly. Kaspar glowered back at his older brother. "Albrecht didn't go to the mainland on business; he left to go back to Germany. He decided there's no money to be made here, but he thinks there is back there. The fool thinks Hitler is saving the place."

Gregor leaned back and sighed. "It's true. Our brother is something of an embarrassment to us right now."

An awkward silence settled over the party until Ana, a determined expression on her face, stood abruptly. "Stop torturing yourselves. It's Saturday night and it's dinnertime, so clear those bottles off the table."

The dinner was, for me, both foreign and delicious: strips of fried iguana, not the fishy-tasting, black marine iguanas but the delicately flavored, camouflage-skinned land iguanas; several kinds of beans; potatoes and tomatoes; a goat stew seasoned to taste almost like lamb; and a slightly tart wine made from cactus flower fruit. By the time we reached dessert—homemade cheese and a selection of both tropical and temperate fruits from the Echeverrías' farm—any discomfort caused by the memory of Albrecht's perfidious behavior had evaporated.

Even before the table had been completely cleared, Kaspar, who had an excellent voice, launched into several German songs, most of which I knew. Héctor replied with several Spanish songs, none of which I knew, although all the Herzogs did. Carla then pulled out her accordion and all hell broke loose as she squeezed the opening notes of a polka. Everybody, both German and Ecuadorean, knew how to polka, and everybody was determined to prove it with everybody else's spouse or date. It took Rojas a few minutes to screw up his nerve, but by the end of the second dance he and Alicia were spinning their way around the house, laughing all the way.

What a strange sight we'd be, I thought in an alcohol-induced flight of fancy, to a person in an airplane above us. Not that I'd ever been in one. A circle of torchlight filled with twisting bodies and swirling dresses and loud singing in Spanish, German, and even a little English.

"Ana," said Carla in a dreamy voice as she allowed herself a short break, "what are they wearing now in New York?" Karen, Luz, and Alicia all leaned forward to listen.

"Women are cutting their hair shorter, and some of their everyday outfits are pretty exciting. They look like the sort of thing we might wear for Carnival."

"I'll visit New York some day."

"You'll find parts of it ugly, just like parts of Naples and Quito. You'll find the rest busy, too busy. There's little beauty there, but a lot is always going on. And there's even more talking and running around than doing."

"Much is happening here, too," mumbled Héctor, thinking perhaps of the agricultural experiments he'd joined Don Vicente de Guzmán in conducting.

By midnight, the rigors of life in Las Encantadas had combined with the food, drink, singing, and dancing to exhaust everybody, leaving Ana and me slouched over the table, side by side, staring out into the pitch-black bay.

"How did you like going to college in New York?" I asked, hoping to keep my new sense of intimacy with her from blowing away in the breeze.

"I liked it. Most of it. There was so much to see and learn. But there were things I really hated. Some of the people, like all the witless boys with too much money and too few manners. The ones who liked to call me 'Banana Princess.'"

I took a deep breath. "Sergeant López insists on calling me 'Fritz.'"

"Does that irritate you?"

"Yes. It's like the Irish calling me 'the Dutchman.' It's not usually intended to be nice."

"López is dangerous. He doesn't bother us, but many people are afraid of him. Do your best to get away from him."

"He was born here, wasn't he? He said he left and came back almost thirty years later."

"According to Roberto, López's father was a former prisoner, like Roberto. The father was killed in a fight and the mother took him to the mainland, and nobody heard anything about him until he returned. The man who was governor then immediately made him his police chief, and every other governor since has done the same. He's become very powerful. I think it has something to do with who he knows ashore, in Quito."

"Do you plan to go back to New York?" I asked, hoping to escape from López's world and return to Ana's.

"Someday, I'm sure, to visit. Probably on business. Papa has all sorts of plans for me, but then he has all sorts of plans for everything. Ecuador is a very old country, but it's also a very new land. Of course you'll go back to New York after you finish seeing the world. Will the police rehire you?"

I took another deep breath. "When I finish seeing the world, I just might go back. But remember, the New York I knew is probably very different from the New York you knew—dances and clean-cut college boys."

"They weren't as clean-cut as they looked. But I do understand you saw parts I never did and never want to."

We sat in silence a few moments, the awareness of her faint smell and gentle breathing overwhelming me. I leaned over to kiss her, but she gently placed her index finger between our lips. "I want to be a modern woman, Fred. I will be a modern woman, but you must remember that I was born into hundreds of years of traditions and rules."

I sighed and leaned back. It was as if Roberto was standing right behind me.

"I like you very much, and I'm very afraid for you. This business with López is especially worrisome." Then, I could have sworn she ruffled my hair gently with her fingertips, only to look away when I turned toward her.

I reviewed with her the details of my investigation so far and my growing suspicion that the murders were just a sideshow, that something more important was in the works.

"You're right that very few people care who killed those three, but there's so much going on that you don't know about. There's no way you can know if the murders are important for some other reason. Few, if any, of the Galapaguinos understand it either. Germany, Peru, the politicians squabbling while the big foreign companies build their oil and mining concessions. Even in Quito very little is clear, not even to those directly involved. They're shadows fighting shadows. Who, for example, does López really work for?"

"The governor."

"Eduardo, the governor, is a decent young guy, but he's also a pitiful fool. He should be back in Quito where his mind might survive. They sent him here because everybody trusts him to do nothing that will threaten them. López takes his orders directly from somebody in Quito. You can bet on that."

"Who?"

"It could be a hundred different people on a dozen different sides. I'm not sure how to find out without spending months there. Not even Papa knows for sure who is who these days, and he knows everybody. We're a very old family."

"You're not being very encouraging."

"I know. I'm sorry. What do you plan to do next?"

"I'm going to see the cook, Elías, again. And Sofía, the maid. I want to know where Ritter and Ernst were when their mistress was killed."

"That makes sense. I hope you want my opinion."

"I do. After I talk to the cook and the maid, I plan to track down Becker and find out exactly how he fits in, no matter what López says."

"I've met him. He's very German, very stiff and arrogant. He's also very handsome in a German way. But he's not as handsome as you."

López wasn't the only person in my life skilled at spinning webs, I thought as I listened to her. "Who is he? What's he doing here? I've seen him once, but he did all the talking and didn't tell me anything. He looks very military."

"He tells people he's a businessman looking for new opportunities. I think he's probably a Nazi, whether or not he's really a businessman."

"He sounded that way to me. Why's López discouraging me from looking for him while the commandant says he wants to know about him?"

"Will you let me help you find out? I'm a Galapaguina, part time anyway, and people sometimes tell me things they might not tell you."

"You're also the daughter of a powerful landowner. Some people don't like telling things to daughters like that."

"None of us is perfect."

"You keep telling me how dangerous all this is, and you're right. I don't want to be doing it. If I could I'd run like hell right now. Why should I let you get involved?"

"All I'll do is listen carefully to what people tell me."

You and Rojas, I thought. Both listening carefully.

13

Dawn must have broken the next morning, but neither I nor any of the others at the party were in any position to swear to it. The first sign of life, after the slow opening of my eyes, was Ana stepping out of Kaspar's house to wash at the sink out back. As she returned to the house she glanced at me lying under a makeshift tent rigged next to the house, and waved. I slid off the cushions I'd been resting on and looked up. It was near noon. My head was pounding, and my mouth was as dry as the Galápagos coast. Then I noticed Don Vicente's launch chugging across the harbor, sharp white waves forming along each of its bows.

I dragged myself to my feet and waited. Ana soon reappeared, carrying her bag, with Carla beside her. Both were laughing. Neither looked any the worse for wear. Carla glanced at me with a wicked smile. She then said something in staccato Spanish to Ana, who glanced at me again, laughed, then replied, again in Spanish. I looked around for Rojas, hoping he was nearby to tell me what they'd said. He wasn't.

Roberto had already maneuvered the launch alongside the dock when we reached it. "I've had a wonderful time, Carla," said Ana as she let me help her aboard. "I'll host the next party." Then, still holding my arm, she pulled me closer and kissed me on the cheek. "I meant everything I said, Fred. Come visit us soon." She stepped back, nodded to Roberto, and the launch pulled away from the dock and headed out to the open ocean.

"Well, Fred," said Carla, "you've made a real impression on that girl."

Ana's kiss was the high point of the day for me. We all managed to choke down a late brunch of fruit, bread, and some leftover stew, then retreated into the shade to continue recuperating. At some point in the afternoon the Echeverrías dragged themselves off to go home. Finally, around four, I decided I'd be able to tolerate a beer. After the second, I began to feel almost human, and by dinner it seemed as if we all would live.

"You plan to visit Blackwater tomorrow?" asked Gregor between mouthfuls of fish and corn.

"Yes, to see the cook again. He knows much more than he told me. And I want to find the maid. One of them must know where Ritter and Ernst were when the baroness was killed."

"If you see Piers Hanson, be careful with him."

"He does have a temper, but he was civil enough to me last time." But not to the little kid, I thought. The one he'd stoned.

"Do you know what happened to his first wife, the one before Christina, back in Norway?"

The question caught me off guard. I hadn't realized Christina was Piers's second wife. "No, do you?"

"Nobody does. Not even Olaf, or so he says. They say she just disappeared."

"What happened to Christina?"

"She's OK," Carla assured me. "I saw her walk aboard the Guayaquil boat."

"You find that Becker fellow and get him out of our islands," exploded Karen, completely out of the blue.

"Do you know him? Why didn't you tell me before?"

"No, I don't know him, but I know he's a Nazi, and he's here to kill a man."

"What?"

"Karen!" sighed Gregor.

"Seven or eight years ago," Karen continued, undeterred, "a high-ranking Nazi official was killed in Munich by a Communist. Or so they say. The official was a close friend of Hitler, and the killer escaped and now lives somewhere here. Becker has been sent to find and kill him. Ask the Crazy German."

"Fred," said Gregor, "Karen's been carried away by this story for some time. The Crazy German got his name because he is."

"He may be, but I believe him," insisted Karen.

"Who is this fellow?" I asked.

"He's an old man who lives by himself in the forest several miles inland from Wreck Bay."

"Maybe I should talk to him."

"Only if you have nothing better to do."

I decided to think about it and, in the meantime, to enhance my cure by going for a swim. The swim did wonders and after another beer I pronounced myself cured. And ready for bed.

The next morning when the gunboat arrived, Rojas and I thanked Carla and Gregor for a wonderful visit and jumped aboard. The skipper must have had a good weekend too, because his normal resentful frown was replaced with a wide smile. Maybe I had one fewer enemy than I did a few days before.

About an hour after leaving Navy Bay, we came across two fishing boats tied together, drifting out in the middle of nowhere. The skipper took the gunboat alongside to make sure they weren't in trouble. They weren't. The fishermen were just chatting, sipping warm beers and taking a break. Piers Hanson had told the truth about at least one thing— the Galapaguinos fished how, where, and when they felt like it.

When we arrived at Blackwater Bay, Elías wasn't hard to find. Even before the gunboat had landed on the beach, we could see and hear him. He was circling Piers Hanson with a knife in his hand, screaming, according to Rojas, that he hated all Germans and was going to cut off Hanson's testicles and then kill him. Hanson, who also had a knife, was shouting that Elías was a filthy pig, and worse. A small crowd of Ecuadoreans had gathered around the two brawlers. According to my assistant, all were rooting for Elías.

Elías looked handy with a knife, but so did Hanson. I didn't want the cook hacked to pieces before I could talk to him, so I grabbed an oar from the sailor who'd rowed us in. Holding it beside me, I mingled with the crowd. The cook and the Norwegian were so focused on each other that neither noticed me.

The two contestants continued circling until Hanson's back was toward me. I swung the oar, caught him on the back of the head, and sent him sprawling. Before Elías could take advantage of the situation, I drew my revolver and pointed it at him. "Tell him to put the knife down," I told Rojas. "Tell him I want to speak to him."

Elías was still filled with rage, and rum, but he had the sense to drop his knife. I looked at Hanson, who was sitting up now. "Get out of here."

Hanson didn't get out of there. He leapt up and crouched, his front covered with sweat and sand and his knife firmly in his right hand. "I'm going to kill you for that," he snarled. "Gut you like a cod." The fury in his eyes was like a flight of spears.

I stared at him, my heart stopping. I was looking down an alley in Hell's Kitchen on a hot July evening, dressed in a wool business suit and tie. Even though the sun had disappeared behind the decaying five- and six-story tenements, I felt like a slab of overcooked beef in a bubbling stew pot, and the gooey asphalt made every step a struggle. An old grocer lay on the cobblestones in the alley, beaten to within an inch of his life, blood burbling out of his smashed mouth. Crouching next to the wrecked grocer was a two-bit punk, a well-known extortion specialist. In his hand was a very big, very sharp knife, and I knew he knew how to use it. My arms and shoulders tensed and, at the same time, felt childishly weak. He was shouting at me, and I understood every word he said yet had no intention of admitting I did. I knew what he was saying, but I didn't care. The sight of the grocer enraged me, making it even more difficult to breathe in the stifling heat. In a fury I fired, then fired again. Both slugs slammed into the punk's chest, and then he was lying on the cobbles beside the grocer, twitching slightly.

I stood for a moment, shaking and gasping for breath. Then I knelt down beside the grocer. He was still alive. I looked up at the surrounding windows, some glinting in the dying sun, and saw no sign of life. I knew there were faces behind the windows, watching. I knew none of them would show themselves. To do so could have been fatal. I stood, turned, and ran out toward the street in search of a call box.

But this time was different. The fear was there, that Hanson might really gut me, despite my revolver, but the fury was lacking. There was no mangled old grocer, just a young cook who was beginning to seem like a punk himself. "I've killed men before, and I won't hesitate to shoot you," I snapped. "Go home."

Hanson looked at the revolver, an element of craftiness replacing the blind rage in his eyes. "You have a gun. I also have a gun, and we will discuss this again someday." He turned and walked toward his house.

"German pigs," translated Rojas as Elías continued to rant. "They tell us what to do and take everything they want."

"He's not German."

"All foreigners are the same. He wanted my cousin to be his whore, and when she refused he beat her up. They take what they want."

"Tell all these people to get back to work," I instructed Rojas. After the crowd had drifted off, I turned back to Elías. "Where were Ritter and Ernst the night the baroness was killed?"

"How would I know?" he demanded.

"Where were they?" I pressed. It was only a hunch, but I felt certain he'd know.

"Up at the shed," he said finally, apparently deciding he had nothing to lose by telling me.

"The one beside the barn?"

"Yes. Whenever the bitch had a visitor for the night, she sent them there."

"She had a visitor that night? Why didn't you tell me before?"

The question caused the cook to pause a moment, as if collecting his thoughts. "I was afraid."

"Of what?"

"You're a German. He's a German and a very violent man."

"Who?"

"The German. The German named Becker."

As he translated, Rojas gave me a strange look.

"How do you know Becker was there?"

"He arrived late in the afternoon, and the bitch sent her two dogs up to the shed. They had dinner, then Sofía and I cleaned up and left. The German was still there."

"Were they arguing?"

"No, they were having fun."

"Where does Sofía live?" I asked, wanting to confirm Elías's tale.

"Up there," he replied, pointing inland. "On the side of the mountain."

"How do I find her house?"

"She's not there. She's gone to visit relatives on Isabela."

"Isabela?"

"Another island, sir," explained Rojas. "The biggest."

"Where on Isabela?"

"I don't know. I wish I did."

"Why do you wish you did?"

He paused a second. "So I could tell you."

Whether or not he really did know, now wasn't the time to pound it out of him. Anyway, up till now I'd found the "good cop" routine was working pretty well.

Damnation! Becker *was* involved, no matter what López kept saying. In fact, he'd suddenly become suspect number one. Now I had to find him.

"Don't go anywhere, Elías," I said after thinking a moment. "I may want to talk to you again."

"I'm not going anywhere. I live here. Do you?"

With Rojas following, I walked down the beach to the boat and returned the oar to the sailor. "Back to the gunboat," I told Rojas. "I want to take another look at the castle and the shed, then back to Wreck Bay."

The gunboat anchored below the castle, and everything looked as it had before. Rojas and I walked up to the patio and paused. The double doors were still shut and the birds still twittering, but something had changed. I opened the door. Ritter's and Ernst's mangled bodies were gone. López must have attended to that. There was still dried blood everywhere, but little else remained besides fragments of the broken chairs and a few other odds and ends. The room had been stripped clean of everything at all useful, as had the kitchen and the small bedroom. Only the baroness's bedroom remained untouched. It was as if the looters believed she'd carried some virulent disease. Or they believed that some sort of evil, supernatural power lurked in that one room.

"I told you before, sir, they're poor people here," remarked Rojas in answer to my unasked question.

"OK, now we take another look at the shed." I glanced one final time around the now-naked room and headed out to the patio.

The hordes of carnivorous flies that had attacked us last time came back for seconds. When we reached the shed, I was angry, bitter, and frustrated, and what we found there did nothing to improve my mood: nothing had changed. "The gun, Rojas."

"The gun, sir?"

"We haven't found it yet."

"It could be anywhere, sir."

"But it might be here. We're going to take the shed and the barn apart, and then search every square foot of the forest nearby."

"How would it get back here?"

"I don't know, but we have to look."

"Yes, sir."

We spent the next hour looking but failed to find any guns or any evidence of one. "Now we do the trail, then the forest around the castle. We'll get the whole gunboat crew on it."

"Yes, sir."

We fought our way back down the trail, examining every inch of forest along each side. "It could be anywhere, sir," groaned my aide. "If the murderer did leave it behind, the people probably found it and took it."

I glowered at him. His logic didn't make me feel any better. "When we reach the castle, you go out in the boat and tell the skipper to bring in all his men except one to help search."

He nodded.

We made it to the castle, and I looked down at the beach. We'd left the boat there with the two oarsmen, but now the beach was empty. Where the hell was the boat?

"Out there, sir."

I followed Rojas's pointing arm and saw the boat out near the gunboat, rowing rapidly toward us. The gunboat skipper was standing on the tiny bridge of his vessel, waving wildly. The instant the boat's bow slid into the rocky sand, the two oarsmen turned and started shouting at Rojas, whose expression changed from hot and tired to shocked.

"The governor has killed himself, sir," reported Rojas, "and the commandant wants us and the gunboat back in Wreck Bay immediately."

14

When we arrived, Wreck Bay was as jammed as it probably ever has been since the departure of the pirate fleets. *Pegasus* and the American schooner were anchored in the center, while a dozen large, well-appointed launches were either anchored around them or moored to the pier. One of the launches was Don Vicente de Guzmán's. The sight of Don Vicente's launch stimulated a surge of energy that coursed through my tired body and unsettled mind. Ana might be here!

I scanned the plaza, hoping to see her. At the same time, I was nervous about what else I might discover. From what I'd seen, the Galapaguinos had neither the time for nor an interest in politics, but events like a governor's death have been known to lead to unexpected results. To my relief, the only sign of anything unusual was two or three sailors standing around the sandy plaza with rifles slung over their shoulders. They looked bored and seemed to be devoting their full attention to leering at the women who occasionally walked by.

The sailor at the naval headquarters reception desk recognized us and waved us into an office. "Hello, Fred," said Ana in a subdued voice. She was sitting behind the desk, looking both irritated and sad at the same time. "*Hola*, Seaman Rojas." She was wearing a black dress and looked very proper.

"Hello, Ana."

"You know about Eduardo, the governor, don't you?"

"The gunboat skipper said he's killed himself. I'm sorry to hear it. He seemed troubled."

"His brain may have been scrambled, but he was neat right to the end. He lay down in his bathtub to avoid making a big mess and slit his wrists." I could see her clenched hands trembling slightly. "They've moved him to the ice factory. They plan to send him to the mainland on the next boat."

"Does this create some sort of a local crisis?"

"I doubt it. No matter what impression López may have given you, the navy really runs things here, and everybody's accustomed to that. The civilian governor is window dressing; he's here because some of the politicians in Quito don't trust the navy. As long as there aren't many problems, the navy lets the governor—or in other words, López—manage the civilians."

"What now?"

"The commandant's in the conference room with half a dozen of the more important landowners discussing the situation."

"And . . . ?"

"And, he asked me to wait here. He's not a bad fellow, and I don't think he'd personally mind my being there, but he doesn't want to offend the more traditional planters and merchants." A note of irritation had crept into her voice.

"Is López in there? I'd expected to find him standing on the pier, waiting to grab me."

"No. I assume he's looking after the governor."

"Will this cost him his job?"

"I doubt it. Remember, there's somebody in Quito who wants him here."

I stared out the window a moment, thinking of the governor as I'd seen him—a man clearly tormented almost to the limit. Beyond his limit, as it now appeared. "Whatever the political significance," I said, "this is very sad. When I met him, the man was suffering. Do you think anybody was putting pressure on him for some reason?"

"No," said Ana with a sigh. As she spoke, she stared at her hands, which were still clasped on the desk in front of her. "And even if they were, he probably wouldn't have noticed. Eduardo always lived more inside his own head than outside it. He wasn't comfortable with reality. I always found him charming but a little too self-conscious. He lacked confidence. We knew him and his family in Quito. He should never have been sent here! The appointment was his death sentence. I can't imagine why he accepted it or why his parents agreed, unless he felt it was the only way he could redeem himself. In fact, they probably went to a lot of trouble to get it for him."

"Why did he need redemption?" I asked with more than casual interest.

"Something about a lost cablegram—an important one, I'm sure, but not the end of the world. And also something about insulting somebody important. Probably accidentally. I'm willing to bet that was his real crime."

At least he didn't shoot and kill the wrong guy, I mused, thinking of my own self-imposed exile to Las Encantadas.

A pained silence settled over the room. I looked closely at Ana and realized there were tears in her eyes. Should I be jealous of the dead governor, I wondered. "Did you know him well?"

"Socially, that's all."

"Go to school with him?"

"No. Papa let the nuns have me, and before you ask, when I was with them I did things their way."

The reception area filled with the sound of voices as the door to the conference room opened and the landowners emerged. All were dressed in business suits and ties with black mourning bands on their arms. A tall, robust gentleman with a full head of auburn hair detached himself from the crowd and walked into the office. "Papa," said Ana, "this is Fred Freiman and Seaman Rojas I told you about."

Don Vicente de Guzmán shook my hand and nodded genially at Rojas. "I very much wish we'd been able to attend the party at the Herzogs' the other night. I'm sure my wife and I would have enjoyed it. According to my daughter," he continued, turning toward Rojas, "Seaman Rojas danced like a madman with Héctor Echeverría's girl."

"She's a very nice girl, sir, and knows many jokes."

"What did the commandant say?" demanded Ana, while Don Vicente and Rojas were still smiling at the memory of the party only one of them had attended.

"Nothing of any significance. He says there's a very slight concern that our Peruvian friends might send a fleet to take over our islands, but that likelihood is too small to even worry about." Don Vicente paused while a sailor came and led Rojas off in the direction of the conference room. "Other than that, he's very sorry that the governor was so unhappy, and we must all remember poor Eduardo as what he was: an honest, honorable, and efficient official and a noble gentleman. The commandant assumes a new governor will be appointed in due course, and in the meantime all will continue as before. I agree with him. Sad though this is, it will have no effect on life in the islands and none on politics in Quito."

Ana didn't exactly dab at her eye, but she did brush it with the back of her hand.

"Then Sergeant López will continue as before?" I asked.

"I assume so," replied Don Vicente.

"Is there any chance it wasn't suicide?"

"A small one, I'm sure," agreed Don Vicente, "but both the commandant and I feel that it was. His valet, who has been with Eduardo's family his entire life, has been very concerned about him for some time. He was with Eduardo not two minutes before it happened and now appears almost suicidal himself. However, if you have some reason to suspect we are wrong, please let me know right away."

"I know even less than you do, sir. I just felt the question should be asked."

"Indeed it should."

The messenger returned to the office and beckoned me to follow him. "Don Vicente," I started, offering my hand.

"No," said Ana, "we'll wait, won't we, Papa?"

Don Vicente looked at her and smiled in a fatherly way. "Of course!" Despite his imposing appearance, he was clearly a pushover when it came to his daughter.

The commandant was seated at the head of the table in the conference room; Rojas stood off to one side. "I understand from Seaman Rojas that you have been a very busy man, Mr. Freiman." The naval officer was speaking English—slowly and with a heavy accent, but he obviously was more fluent than he had let on at our last meeting. "He tells me you have not yet managed to identify the killer, or killers, but that you now have a reason to suspect that Herr Becker might be involved in some way."

Speaking slowly and as carefully as I could, I reviewed whom I'd spoken with and what I'd learned. Being unsure of the true nature of the relationship between the commandant and the sergeant, I made a point of not mentioning that López seemed intent on guiding me away from Becker, but I needn't have been cautious—it seemed the commandant was already aware of my suspicions.

"Yes, it is a very complex situation. I understand from Rojas that you feel Sergeant López does not want you to look for Becker." As he spoke I noted a tone of distaste in his voice. Whether it was for the German or the sergeant I couldn't tell.

I glanced at Rojas and felt sorry for him. How many people could one young sailor report to and work for all at the same time without, in the end, hanging himself?

"I may just misunderstand his desires, sir."

The commandant smiled slightly. "Please understand, Mr. Freiman, it is very much my desire that you locate this man Becker and determine for certain what he is doing. I am sure you understand by now that the situation in my country is every bit as complicated as that of the world at large. There are tensions between the armed forces and the civilian politicians, between the businessmen and the workers, between the aristocrats and the new industrialists, between those who wish to see Ecuador work with you North Americans and those who want to work with the Germans. It is easy to think of these islands as a forgotten corner of the world, a place of no significance. But I am certain that both Washington and Berlin have their eyes on us. Do we understand each other?"

"We do, sir. Will you let Rojas continue to work with me?"

"Of course."

"Sir?" I wasn't sure I really wanted to ask the question. Or even if I should.

"Yes, Mr. Freiman?"

"Is it possible that the governor's unhappiness—depression—was more than a matter of his basic temperament? Could he have been worried about something else? Something specific?"

The commandant smiled grimly. "The governor's life was in Quito, and he was stuck out here. His career was in danger, and he is known to have been melancholic all his life. I also think he resented the power Sergeant López has acquired over the years. But to answer your real question, I have seen no suggestion that he was taking bribes or betraying the Republic or doing anything else dishonorable. It is always possible that I have not seen everything I should. I would be saddened and surprised, but not angry with you, if you come across something I don't know."

"Did he have any business interests out here?"

"His only interest was in going home."

"Any love interests?"

The commandant laughed. "No. Everybody would have known if he did. There is little privacy here."

When we returned to the office, Rojas and I found Ana still sitting behind the desk while Don Vicente paced back and forth. "What did he want?" asked Ana.

"Same as before. He wants me to find out what Becker's doing."

"Do you know where he is?"

"No, and I'm not even sure at this point where to start looking. I saw him here, in Wreck Bay, a few days ago, and nobody admits to having seen him since. But López may be willing to help me find him now that I know Becker was with the baroness the night she was killed."

"Really? How do you know that?"

"Because he was seen there," I explained, wondering if maybe I was talking too much.

"Maybe we should talk to the Crazy German," offered Rojas. "Señora Herzog said she thinks he might know something about Becker."

I looked at the seaman, then at Ana.

"It's a starting point," she agreed. "He may know something useful about Becker. You just said you don't know where to start."

Don Vicente, who'd stopped pacing and was perched on the corner of the desk with his arms folded, suddenly looked very uncomfortable. "That man is truly insane," he said.

"But not really dangerous," insisted Ana. "I know where he lives. He's hard to find. I'll take you there."

Don Vicente's expression changed from discomfort to outright concern as he stared at his daughter. "How do you know that?"

"Roberto and I get around, usually on some business for you."

Don Vicente grunted. Serves him right, I thought, for raising her to be a modern woman. I wondered what her mother thought of it all. "Thanks," I finally said, "but not today. I think I'd better find López and tell him about Becker's connection to the murders."

"That's very wise, Fred," said Don Vicente before Ana could say another word. "I understand that the commandant wants you to locate this German, but you must understand that his may not be the last word out here. López has powerful backers in Quito, and the navy may not be the most powerful force there. Come, Ana, perhaps we should get home."

At first Ana looked as if she was going to argue, but then she thought better of it. "Radio me when you want to go see the Crazy German. Roberto can bring me to Wreck Bay."

Don Vicente smiled slightly and shrugged his shoulders. It wasn't a shrug of defeat but one of acceptance and even satisfaction. He'd set out to raise his daughter to standards that differed from those of his class. And he'd succeeded. Now all he had to do was worry that he might have made a mistake. Or gone too far. "I'm very serious, Fred, when I say I hope you'll come visit us soon," he said as he offered his hand. "My wife will find you charming, and I think you'll find our plantation of great interest."

I watched them walk out the door toward the pier. "Seaman Rojas," I asked, "is there a telephone line from here to the ice factory?"

"Yes, sir, one of the few on the island."

"Good. I want to call Sergeant López and arrange to meet with him."

My aide led me back to the vestibule where one extension of the island's very limited telephone system sat on the desk. Rojas placed the call, listened a moment, then said *gracias* and hung up. "The sergeant's not there, sir. He delivered the governor's body and then left, and they don't know where he went."

"He's probably headed back here," I reasoned. "We'll wait for him."

15

Two hours later López still hadn't appeared and, sitting in a more or less enclosed room, I was very aware of how much I smelled. "Rojas, we both could use a bath and a change of clothes, so I am going out to my boat and you may wish to use the facilities here."

"I'm sure you're welcome to use our showers, sir."

"Thank you, but I'll return to *Pegasus*. You come out in two hours so we can plan our next move. And find a few beers to bring along. Here's some money."

Rojas took the money, and I walked down to the pier and jumped into my dinghy just as the sun started to kiss the horizon. There was nothing wrong with the navy's showers—a little old and moldy, perhaps—but I wanted some privacy. It may sound ridiculous to complain about a lack of privacy in a sparsely populated assemblage of volcanic rocks in the middle of nowhere, but the commandant was right. Between López, the commandant, and some of the stranger residents, I was beginning to feel as closed in as I had on that steaming July evening in Hell's Kitchen.

I reached *Pegasus*, stripped, and jumped over the side with what was left of my saltwater soap, in a hurry to complete the job before the sun totally disappeared. Although I hadn't yet spotted one, the bay was said to have a large shark population and, as everybody knows, they tend to be more active at night. Despite my shark worries, the dark-blue, almost-cold water was so refreshing that I let myself float a few moments. All thoughts of dead baronesses, crazy Germans, suicidal Ecuadorean aristocrats, and police sergeants who weren't really police floated away with the soap scum. I climbed back aboard *Pegasus* and, after checking that the navy had filled my water tanks, drew a bucket of freshwater and rinsed, dried myself, and slipped into clean trousers and shirt. I then settled into the cockpit and watched as the last rays of the sun bathed the settlement. At high noon Wreck Bay looked as utterly shopworn as it really was, yet now, in the last mellow light of the day, it could have been El Dorado.

My thoughts turned to more pressing topics, specifically that Ana might manage somehow to get hurt by being involved with me. Two hours ago my biggest worry had been that I was trapped in a political situation I had no means of understanding, but now the threat seemed much more solid, immediate, and personal. Three people had already been murdered, and I still had no idea why, although I had a number of suspects. If three were already dead, then more could follow. Including Ana and me. I was a total stranger in these strangest of islands and doubted I had any dependable allies, except possibly Ana. And, hopefully, her father. Strangely, I also found Rojas on my list of allies, despite his compelled allegiance to both López and the commandant.

If I failed to produce a murderer satisfactory to López then I would be tried as the murderer. Leaving all personal considerations aside, I couldn't help but believe that whatever was going on was much bigger than just the murder of three very strange Germans. War seemed likely in Europe and almost equally possible in the Pacific, and the commandant's words had succeeded in convincing me that it would probably reach as far as Las Encantadas. And even if the Germans—those that weren't already living here—didn't attack, the Peruvians might take advantage of the confusion to do so themselves.

I felt a bump as a boat came alongside. "It's me, Mr. Freiman, Rojas. I have a case of beer here."

I jumped up and leaned over the side. There was Rojas in a boat with a case of beer and another sailor at the oars. "Excellent!" I shouted. "Pass it up." Within seconds, both the case of beer and Rojas were safely parked in the cockpit. "Wait," I said as Rojas started to say something to the seaman in the boat. "I bet he'd like a beer."

Rojas relayed the offer, and the seaman just smiled as he continued to hang on to *Pegasus*'s rail. I slid below and rooted through the galley drawer for a bottle opener. Call it a bribe if you want or call it simple graciousness, but the Ecuadorean sailors, even the gunboat skipper, had done a lot for me, and gone through a lot, and done so with much less outright grumbling than I used to hear in the New York station house. I wanted them to continue to think kindly of me. While the sailor in the rowboat savored the beer, I opened two more and pulled out a couple cigars that López had provided, either in a fit of generosity or in an effort to bribe me. Rojas accepted a warm beer but passed on the cigar. I watched as the sailor handed the empty bottle up to Rojas, said "thank you, sir" in English, then rowed off into the night. I lay back, placing my head against the cabin bulkhead, and looked up into the night.

The jet-black sky was now almost hidden by a brilliant almost-solid mass of silver-blue stars, and the wind was blowing gently but steadily. I could, I thought, send Rojas ashore in my dinghy, heave up the anchor, and be well underway before midnight. But I knew I wouldn't. I didn't worry that the commandant would chase me. In fact, I didn't worry about him at all. He was, I concluded, a reasonable man. He might well have the power to have me shot at any time, but he would do so only for a good reason. López, on the other hand, continued to scare me to death. And I still wasn't really sure why. He'd trapped me and manipulated me and threatened me, but those were just common cop tactics. There was something more, something hidden. So many of the islanders didn't just hate him, they feared him. Even, perhaps, the late governor. Yet the reason wasn't obvious, which made it all the more frightening. The commandant wouldn't bother to chase me, but López sure as hell would.

And, if it weren't for López, I wouldn't have even considered leaving. Las Encantadas were beginning to grow on me. Their strange, austere beauty, their almost infinite variety, the sense of openness and of being on a frontier. At the edge of the world or maybe even of the universe. Even the people, the mishmash of northern Europeans and Ecuadoreans. And one of those people in particular: Ana de Guzmán. The smell of her hair in a gentle breeze, the faint tickle of her breath on my cheek, the awareness of a powerful electricity not only when I was close to her but whenever she was in sight—or even in my mind. I was at least ten years older than she. She was part of a very wealthy family and had gone to college. I could claim neither. Yet she acted as if it didn't make any difference to her. It might in Quito, but not here. I loved her sense of adventure, and yet it worried me. It was bound to get her in trouble some day.

I glanced at Rojas's shadowy form. He seemed to be staring up at the stars, too. "We've gotten ourselves into a very difficult position," I observed.

"Sir?"

"I'm trapped between the commandant and López. And there's more, I'm certain. Something's going on around us. Something much bigger than either of them. And if I'm trapped, then I'm afraid you are too."

Rojas sighed and took a sip of his beer. "I'm not an investigator, sir, but I think you're right."

"And I think it has something to do with the Germans. The ones in Germany."

"There are those in the government who favor Germany. And there are many Germans living here. But I don't see the connection between the baroness and her men and whatever is going on. Except that they were Germans."

"Neither do I, but this Becker fellow seems to make some sort of connection." I sat up, stuffed my empty bottle back in the case, and pulled out a full one.

"Then you really did believe Elías?"

"Yes, why shouldn't I?"

"He doesn't have the best reputation."

"Why didn't you tell me before?"

"Because it's mostly rumors."

"Have you ever met Becker?"

"No, sir."

"Seen him?"

"No, sir."

"I've seen him. Talked to him briefly. He looks like a soldier, like the ones you sometimes see in the newspapers, and he does talk like a Nazi. About reshaping the world and getting rid of people who need to be gotten rid of."

"Then you know him."

"I'm acquainted with him. So you don't think this has to do with Germany and the war?"

"It may, sir, but you're overlooking your own people, the North Americans."

"What do you mean?"

"That man you spoke with the other morning, the one with the big sailboat."

"What about him?"

"He's been seen all over the islands."

"He says he's a tourist. Looking at the animals and the scenery."

"He's been seen many times ashore with measuring instruments."

"Measuring instruments?"

"To measure the land."

"Surveying instruments?"

"Yes, that's the word. And he and his men have also been seen collecting rocks."

"Are you blowing smoke in my face? Trying to confuse me?"

"No, sir."

"Do López and the commandant know about all this with Thompson?"

"Yes, sir. I'm sure they both do. It's been talked about at naval headquarters."

"And?"

"The commandant doesn't seem worried. I have no idea how Sergeant López feels about it."

I noticed that the breeze was picking up. I could be away and gone in no time. I could pick up Ana on my way west, to Tahiti, where life would have to be simpler than it was here. Except they speak French in Tahiti. I'd still be an outsider.

"You ready for another beer?"

"Yes, sir. Thank you. Some of what's going on makes me very nervous."

"That makes two of us. Let's go ashore and find some food."

"The navy mess, sir?"

"No, how about that place where we had breakfast? The Miramar?"

"There'll be many interesting people there at night, sir. It's very popular." He then handed me a wad of sucres. "From the commandant, sir. He figured that you must have spent the money López gave you by now."

"And he's undoubtedly worried I won't feed you properly."

"The navy is supposed to feed its sailors, sir."

"One more thing."

"Yes, sir?"

"My Spanish lessons start tonight. You'll be the teacher. We'll concentrate on useful stuff. For example, how do you say 'beautiful'?"

"There are many words for that. Do you mean a beautiful flower or a beautiful ship or a beautiful young doña?" Obviously the kid didn't have a head for alcohol. Either that or he'd totally lost all sense of his place in the world.

"While we're on the subject, Seaman, what exactly is the deal about dons and doñas? I heard you address Ana as 'Doña' the other night. Does that mean her father's a knight or something?"

"It's looser than that, sir. It's a title of respect that you can use with anybody. A teacher, your boss, anybody who's respected or who has authority. Don Vicente, for example, is respected not only because he's very wealthy but also because he's clever and generous. Many of the Galapaguinos seem to feel the same about Doña Ana."

"López never calls her that. He keeps calling her señorita."

"There's nothing wrong with señorita. Or with señora. Alicia Echeverría is a very wonderful señorita. When I'm older I look forward to being a señor. But in this situation, López is being insulting."

"Very well. Which of the 'beautifuls' do you recommend? Tell me and we'll work on the pronunciation on our way to the Miramar."

"I think 'encantadora' is most appropriate."

"Like these islands?"

"If you like."

16

As Rojas had predicted, the Miramar was jumping when we arrived. Every night, it seemed, was Saturday night there. The tables were all taken, and a small but very loud combo—a couple guitars, a trumpet, and a drummer—was pumping out music under the stars. A few couples were strutting around the sandy dance floor, but most of the customers were men who were concentrating on drinking and talking. The women, both those dancing and those sitting at tables, looked tired and worn. I suspected many were there on business.

"These girls . . ." I said to Rojas.

"This is a small settlement, sir. There aren't many, and they all work for the sergeant, so you should be careful what you say around them."

"López?"

"Yes, sir." As Rojas spoke the expression on his face drifted into a frown. Perhaps he was having second thoughts about mentioning López's side business, even if it probably was common knowledge to everybody but me.

I looked again at the girls. I'd had plenty of contact with such women over the years in New York, and I felt a real sympathy for them. I wasn't one of those cops who snarled publicly about "immoral, godless, diseased whores" only to shake them down in private. I'd found a few to be vicious and still more who had become cynical, but many, if not most, were, at heart, sad, discouraged, and resigned. Some were even supporting families. Any job, they seemed to feel, was better than none. The government and the newspapers kept saying everything was getting better, but that would have been hard to prove on the streets and in the alleys of Hell's Kitchen.

"I gather you liked the Echeverría girl," I remarked, hoping to move my thoughts into a more positive realm.

"I did, sir. She reminded me of some of the girls I knew back home. A little more rustic but, I think, smarter."

I looked around the "dining room," which was open to the sky and bordered on the water side by a string of lanterns strung between tall poles and swaying in the misty sea breeze. The night air was filled with the smells of sizzling coconut oil and burning meat, mixed with the tang of the sea and of still-cooling rock. A few of the other patrons glanced at us, but most concentrated on eating, drinking, and talking. I can't say they looked like everybody who was anybody at Wreck Bay—I suspected that the true upper crust wouldn't be caught dead here—but they looked prosperous by island standards. "I don't see any place to sit," I said unhappily. I was hungry.

"He'll find a place for us," my guide assured me, nodding at a small man, dressed in a white shirt and trousers, who was hurrying toward us.

"Good evening, sir," said the man in slow but careful English. "You are the friend of Sergeant López, no?"

I nodded.

"And you wish to eat?"

"Yes, very much."

"Of course!" He then disappeared into the crowd, only to return almost immediately and lead us to the open side overlooking the dark water, where a new table and chairs were being set up under one of the lanterns. "A waiter will be with you very soon." He disappeared again.

"Do you see, sir, you're a very important person here at Wreck Bay." As Rojas said it, he looked as if he were about to burst into one of his incomprehensible fits of laughter. Somehow he managed to control himself.

"As I reminded you on my boat, Seaman Rojas, we're both in the same position. You, therefore, must also be a very important person. And remember, important persons make big, easy targets when the shooting starts."

This time he did laugh, confident now that it was permitted. Then, after thinking about what I'd said, he stopped laughing so hard.

While we were waiting for our meal, Thompson, the American with the big schooner and the big mouth, showed up, a big glass of rum in his hand. He was wearing the same jeans I'd seen him in before, but now he had a flowered sport shirt on. Even in the Galápagos, people dress up when they go out on the town. "Why, it's the American who works for Sergeant López!"

"Hi," I replied, looking up at him and almost shouting to be heard over the combo. I can't say he was drunk, but he didn't look totally sober, either.

Thompson looked pointedly at Rojas, and the young sailor started to stand to give him his chair. "Stay where you are, Rojas," I said. "Our food'll soon be here. I'll get our host to find us another chair."

"Don't bother," said Thompson as I stood to flag down the owner, "I've just got a couple questions."

"Shoot!"

"What's the real story on the governor?" he demanded. "These people seem to tell you more than they're willing to tell me." From the expression on his face he took being left out as a personal insult.

"The real story is that he was a sad case. He couldn't stand this place and wanted to go home."

"Then he really did kill himself?"

"That's what they say. I haven't seen the body or talked to his valet, but I did meet him once, and I believe it."

The combo finished the tune it was playing with a crash and fell momentarily silent.

"Who's in charge around here now?"

"The naval commandant. He always has been, as I understand it. The governor was just window dressing."

"What about López?"

"That's a good question. They say it's complicated, something about who knows who back on the mainland, in the capital."

Thompson had the bad habit of looking at you as if you were an idiot when you told him something he didn't like or understand. But I decided to overlook this shortcoming.

"Why are you really here?" he continued, his expression as suspicious as it was harsh.

"I'm an adventurer, a traveler, just like you. I set out for Tahiti, and this is as far as I've gotten."

"Why's an American working for López?"

"Because he's made it worth my while. You don't like him?"

"No, and I don't trust him, either. He's trouble for us. Where is he, by the way?"

"I'd like to know that myself. Has he given you any trouble?" I asked, my interest growing.

The American frowned, then took another belt of his rum. "Not so far, but I can feel it coming."

"Are you doing something he won't like?"

"Just taking in the sights. Like you. You sure you're on the right side?"

"Of what?"

"There's a war coming, pal. You with us, or are you one of those Bund Krauts who run off to the woods on the weekends so they can shout '*Sieg Heil*' at each other?"

I'd known one or two New World Nazis, but I wasn't one of them, and this guy was beginning to get on my nerves. I started to tell him to go to hell—worse, actually—but then remembered what Rojas had said about his being seen surveying various islands and collecting rocks.

Collecting rocks, I thought. Perhaps the very rocks I'd seen at the castle. And Thompson had been seen at the castle the very day the baroness was killed. Thompson and Becker. Both had been at the castle that day, and both were now wandering around, looking for something. I might learn more from Thompson if I was more polite than he was. I just had to give it a little time. "Bob, no matter what my last name is, I'm an American and on the side of the United States. López asked me to help him solve these murders because I speak German and he doesn't and all the victims and most of the suspects are Germans." There was no reason to add that López was forcing me to do the work, and it didn't seem the right time to tell him he was now at the top of the list of suspects, even though he wasn't German. At least not as far as I could see.

"You just remember whose side you're on," he said. He downed a mouthful of rum, nodded, and sauntered away in the direction of the bar.

"Finally," sighed Rojas as our food arrived.

17

I was up early the next morning. Rojas and I had work to do. I looked over the stern at the rudder and noticed a school of minnows fluttering around and nibbling at the greenery growing on *Pegasus*'s bottom. I was going to have to take time soon to scrub the hull as best I could. Eventually I'd have to somehow haul the boat to give it a good cleaning.

I stripped, then looked out over the bay. There were undoubtedly sharks out there, at least one, but I was able to convince myself that they only attack at night. I quickly plunged over the side into the cool, blue water and scrubbed myself from top to bottom. I floated for a few minutes, enjoying the sense of freedom and weightlessness. I then hauled myself up the swim ladder, dried, and dressed. By the time I reached the pier, my assistant was already waiting there.

The previous evening, after Thompson finished evaluating my loyalty, Rojas and I had decided that now was the time to track down the Crazy German. I wanted to do it before López showed up and told us not to.

"You find out anything useful?" I asked as I tied the dinghy to the pier.

"The name of a man who can tell us how to find the Crazy German."

"What about López?" It's not that I wanted to find him at the moment. Or him to find me. I just wanted to know where he was.

"Nobody seems to know, sir."

I looked around the anchorage. "The gunboat's still here, so he must still be on Santa Cruz."

"Not necessarily, sir. He has another launch that he uses from time to time. He keeps it at the governor's mansion. His office is there, on the first floor in the back, where all the official records are stored."

I looked at him a moment. I already knew about the sergeant's office, but this was the first I'd heard about the launch. I wondered if the seaman had failed to mention it in the past because he wanted to hide it from me or just because I'd never asked. I wondered what else I should know but didn't. I wondered if my feelings of isolation were leading to an excess of paranoia.

"Walk over to naval headquarters and call the governor's mansion. Find out if the launch is still there. For that matter, find out if López is there."

I watched Rojas walk across the sand to the stone headquarters, then turned my attention to the morning soccer game in the plaza. Six boys in all, none older than about ten as far as I could tell, were yelling, waving, weaving, and dancing around the open sand while passersby were forced to weave and dance to keep out of their way. One, the smallest player, put in everything he had and gave the ball a mighty kick. The ball rocketed forward and sailed through the goal, which was marked on the sand. I clapped along with all the players. Then, without warning, they started doing somersaults, although some had a little trouble getting over. I clapped again, not at all certain I could still do a respectable somersault.

I watched them rolling around in the damp sand and thought back to being a kid and to the freedom from reality that kids enjoy. Whatever their future, they were able to concentrate on what was important now—kicking the ball and doing somersaults. I mourned the freedom I'd lost over the years.

Rojas returned a few minutes later. "The launch isn't there, sir. Neither is the sergeant."

"OK. Let's get some food, and then we'll go find the Crazy German."

"I've eaten, sir."

"I'm sure you can choke down a cup of coffee."

"Galápagos coffee is very good, don't you think?"

The breakfast crowd at the Miramar was small and muted. While we waited for my food and Rojas's coffee to appear, I started my Spanish lessons by holding up a knife. "What's this?"

"*Un cuchillo.*"

"*Cuchillo.*" I tried it several times, then went on to fork and spoon and cup and plate. By the time I'd finished counting out the money to pay our bill, we'd also gone over the words for eggs, pork, bread, and oranges.

It didn't take us long to find Humberto, the butcher who Rojas had been told knew how to find the Crazy German. When we arrived at his small shop on one of the settlement's sandy alleys, we found him hard at work gutting and bleeding a pig that hung from the ceiling. Unfortunately, as it turned out, Humberto wasn't totally sane himself. Or sober for that matter, even though the sun was still low in the sky. His directions were a little cloudy.

I wondered if maybe I should've taken Ana's advice and asked her to show us the way, but I was in a hurry and also a little worried about putting her in danger. She might be a modern woman, but I wasn't sure I was a totally modern man. Without Ana to help us, however, we were far from certain we really knew where we were going when we set off down the path Humberto told us to follow inland.

The hike was damn unpleasant. While the land behind Wreck Bay did slowly rise, it failed to achieve the lushness of the highlands of Floreana, and the paper-thin rubber soles of my shoes did nothing to protect my feet from the sharp stones. We marched under the powerful equatorial sun, attacked by swarms of hunger-maddened horseflies. With the exception of the flies and a few alert, clever little lizards, we saw few signs of animal life. Not even a feral goat or one of the huge land tortoises that everybody kept telling me to look for. Most of the time we were guessing where we were going. Fortunately we stumbled across one or two small, sun-dried farms whose lethargic owners directed us.

We found the Crazy German in an incredibly filthy, tumbledown hovel that was protected from the sun by two or three stunted, half-dead trees under which a few scrawny goats were tethered. Off to one side a small vegetable garden wilted while several dozen chickens wandered aimlessly, pecking at the sand and rocks. I can't imagine what the goats and chickens ever found to eat. Our host, a shriveled, bent old man dressed in a pair of tattered shorts and nothing else, was standing in the doorway. He shouted something in Spanish.

"He wants to know what we want," translated Rojas.

I answered in German that I wanted to ask him about a rumor I'd heard. I made no mention of working for López, since he seemed the sort who might not like the sergeant.

"What rumor?" he continued in German.

"About a man who lives someplace in the islands and is hiding from the Nazis."

I figured he'd deny any knowledge of such a thing, but he didn't. Instead, a grimace appeared on his face, a grimace that I later realized was a smile. "Are you a German? Do you now live here?"

"I'm an American. I'm just visiting."

"Come. Yes, come," he said, nodding and beckoning us forward. "I'm cooking my stew for dinner. I will tell you about that man, just as I told the other German a few weeks ago."

Becker, I thought. Who else?

He led us through his one-room shack—a table with two chairs, a filthy bed, a pair of trousers, two ragbag shirts hanging on rusty nails, and three chickens patrolling the dirt floor—and then out the back. There he had another table and a rough stone hearth. I glanced at Rojas, who looked as wilted as the vegetables. "May we have some water?"

"Of course," he replied. He grabbed a food-encrusted tea cup that was decorated with some sort of flower pattern and had no handle, and dipped it in a water-filled oil drum. He offered the cup to me, but I nodded toward my assistant. Rojas accepted the cup and looked at it with distaste. But he was as parched as I was, so, with what was clearly an exercise of will, he drank it. The German refilled the cup and passed it to me, and I followed Rojas's example, closing my eyes and hoping for the best.

"Now let me tell you about that man," said the Crazy German as he stirred the unsavory-looking contents of an iron pot hanging over the half-dead fire.

"Yes," I said, "please do." I spotted a small area of shade right up next to the side of the shack and edged into it.

"He's a Jew and a Communist, and the Nazi thugs were out to kill him because they believed he was a leader of those who wanted to end the Nazis. Because they thought he was important, a very senior SS *Gruppenführer* was put in charge of capturing him and learning what he knew. You know the SS? The Schutzstaffel? Hard men. Vicious men. Killers and torturers. Yes? Well, this man we're talking about was no fool, and he managed to kill the *Gruppenführer* before the *Gruppenführer* was able to capture him. Right there in the center of Munich. He did it with a hunting rifle. From the roof of a building. The *Gruppenführer* was a favorite of Hitler's, so Himmler, the head of the SS, swore to catch him. The man escaped from Germany and ended up here. Himmler somehow learned that he might be here, but he's not sure so the man continues to hide. Few of us know who he is or where he is, but he's here."

"Do you know this man? Have you ever seen him?"

"He's here somewhere."

"What did you tell the other German who came to visit you?"

"Just what I'm telling you." He then leaned over the pot of stew, hawked, and spat into it. Several times. "That improves the flavor. Stay and have some with me."

"Do you know who the other German is who asked you about this?"

"Yes. A Nazi. Are you?"

"No. I'm an American. If the other German is a Nazi, why did you tell him about this man?"

"Because I'm afraid of the SS. If I cooperate maybe they'll leave me alone. Why do you look for the man who killed the SS *Gruppenführer*?"

"I'm not looking for him. I want to find the other German. Was he looking for the man who killed the SS officer?"

"The Nazi?"

"If that's what he is."

"No. He was just walking around, looking at the rocks. I told him about the man who killed the *Gruppenführer*. He is here, someplace. Please stay and have dinner with me. People tell me my stew is excellent."

"That would be an honor and a pleasure, but we must get back to Wreck Bay. This business about the governor is causing confusion."

"What about the governor?"

"He killed himself a few days ago."

"Nobody ever tells me anything."

The hike back to Wreck Bay was just as brutal as the trip out. As we cursed and flailed wildly at the hungry flies, I explained to Rojas what the Crazy German had said.

"Do you believe him, sir? Perhaps there's a reason he's called crazy."

"I don't know."

When we reached Wreck Bay I returned immediately to *Pegasus* so I could strip and plunge once more into the heavenly cool water. The result was a near miracle. The massive welts left by the flies no longer itched maddeningly, although they did sting a little. I pulled myself up the swim ladder, rinsed off in freshwater, and settled down in the cockpit to enjoy a lukewarm beer while I air-dried in the evening light.

Everywhere I looked in Las Encantadas there were people who had, or thought they had, at least one good reason to kill the baroness. I had far too many suspects with good motives. I also had two suspects, Becker and Thompson, who were seen at the castle the day of the murder but who lacked any obvious motive. Except possibly inflamed passion. The baroness seemed to have a powerful effect on everybody she met, although different men seemed to see very different things in her. Or could politics have been a factor? Could Becker really be an SS officer and the baroness an enemy of the German state?

I dressed and rowed in to the dock, where Rojas was waiting for me. I'd considered giving him the night off and going out to dinner by myself, but decided against it. Anyway, he didn't seem to have the slightest objection to our joint dining expeditions. We went back to the Miramar. It was crowded, but it was also early so the crowd wasn't as thick, or as drunk. After García, the *patrón*, had seated us and a waiter had taken our order for beers, I settled back to listen to the combo.

"Fritz, they tell me you're becoming a regular here."

I almost jumped out of my chair, then turned and found López looking down at me, a beer bottle in one hand.

"I've been working hard for you, Sergeant."

"So I hear," said López as he glared at Rojas. "Seaman, leave us for a few minutes. When you see me leave you may return."

Rojas leapt out of the chair and disappeared in the direction of the bar.

"Do you have a name for me, Fritz? Somebody I can send to the mainland?"

"I've got half a dozen, but I can't prove any of them guilty."

"Is that really important in the situation you're in?"

"Even in this situation I'd like to finger the guilty party."

"Finger? Yes, finger. Keep at it."

"About Becker—"

"Becker didn't do it. I don't want you to waste your time on him."

"What do you know about Thompson, the American with a big schooner?"

"What about him?"

"He admits he was at the castle and saw the baroness the day she was killed."

"Really? Good. That would be very tidy. There are many in Quito who would be very happy to see a Yanqui in prison for murder." I wondered if he meant Thompson or me. "See if you can get anything definite. And remember, while the governor's weakness was unfortunate, it changes nothing. You still work for me, not for the commandant, as you may have been led to believe. I'm the person who will decide who is sent to the mainland to stand trial for the murders."

"And when I finger somebody for you, you'll let somebody fix my engine?"

"I'll have the navy look at it. I suspect you'll have to order a new one from the mainland."

"I understand."

"Then also understand that I've known who you are since the day after you arrived. I radioed friends on the mainland who telegraphed other friends in New York. You shot and killed a gangster who was protected by an agreement between the Mob and certain police officers. Both of them would like to talk to you. If you return to the United States, you're a dead man. If I tell them you're here, you're a dead man. Now we truly understand each other, no?"

Before I could utter the most pitiful squawk, before my heart could start beating again, the sergeant had stood and walked off.

18

As López sauntered off into the crowd, the waiter immediately appeared with our meals. Within seconds, Rojas was back and seated.

"How is Sergeant López, sir?"

"Right up to his usual standards. You got back to the table very quickly."

"I'm very hungry, sir. Did you tell him we saw the Crazy German?"

"No. When are you next supposed to report to him?"

"There's no schedule, sir. He comes to me when he wants to ask questions. Or he has me come to him."

"Well for God's sake don't lie to him."

"I'll try to avoid him, sir."

"Good. Let's enjoy our dinner while we can."

We were about halfway through our meal—Rojas had beef and I had roast chicken and tried not to think about the Crazy German's stew—when I realized my assistant was looking over my shoulder. "Excuse me," said a voice in very slow and careful English. I turned, but before I could reply, Rojas had launched into a brief discussion in Spanish.

"My friend Gonzales here has been sent to deliver a radio message to you, sir."

The uniformed messenger looked to be just about the same age as Rojas. He also looked a little uncomfortable at his position, but not seriously so. "Please," I said, holding out my hand.

Gonzales smiled and handed me an envelope. I opened it and found the message, as advertised, but it was in Spanish. I handed it to Rojas. "It's from Doña Ana de Guzmán, sir, and it says, 'It took me a long time, and many arguments, but my father finally agreed to let you come visit us. Please come just as soon as you can.'"

"What?" I mumbled. How could there have been an argument? Don Vicente had made it very clear that he wanted me to visit.

"I think the doña likes you, sir," said Rojas, trying to control a smile.

This kid is on the border of getting out of control again, I thought.

I looked at Gonzales and thought how well a little generosity and good cheer seemed to work in Las Encantadas. "Would your friend like a beer or something to eat?" What better way to spend López's money? Or was I using the commandant's money now?

"I'm sure he would, sir, but he's on duty and there are people here who might say something to our superiors, so he'll just say thank you but no. Do you wish to reply to the message?"

"Yes."

Rojas nodded, and Gonzales handed me a blank message form and a pencil, which I handed to Rojas. "Tell her 'Excellent, I'll try to come tomorrow.'"

Rojas wrote and returned the message to Gonzales, who then disappeared into the crowd. "How did the commandant know we're here?"

"Sergeant López isn't the only person who has friends all over the settlement, sir."

"The commandant will already know about the messages. When will you tell López?"

"When he asks, sir, but I doubt I'll see him again before we leave in the morning."

"What makes you think I plan to take you with me this time?"

"I've tried to be very useful, sir."

"And you have been, but you're also a spy. For two different people."

"Not a very good one, sir. I tell Sergeant López less than I tell the commandant, and there are many things I don't tell him."

"You could get yourself shot."

"I doubt that, sir. Not shot. I'm only a common seaman."

"Did you understand what that message really meant?"

"That she wants to see you, sir. I was a little confused since Don Vicente seemed to like you."

"I like to think that."

"Then she's trying to tell you to hurry. Maybe she has something to show you."

"Or somebody."

"I would like to see Don Vicente's plantation, sir. Everybody says he's doing all sorts of wondrous things out there. I may learn something that will be of use to me after I leave the navy."

I realized then that Rojas, if he managed to survive his association with me, would grow up to be a politician. Or some other kind of con man.

After we finished eating, I sent Rojas to inform the gunboat skipper that, unless the commandant ordered otherwise, we'd be getting under way at first light. Then I noticed what looked like López's bike parked outside the entrance. I felt the engine. It was cool. I looked around and didn't see him, so I ducked back into the restaurant and still couldn't find him. He had to be there someplace, but there was no reason to look for him now. He'd already delivered his message for the night. On my way out again I stopped and looked at the motorcycle. It was a German DKW. I knew they made good machines. I'd considered buying one a few years ago but decided it wasn't worth the cost since Alf was always willing to lend me his car.

López had already ruined my night, and thinking about Alf ground it into my face. I decided not to return to *Pegasus* right away. Instead, I'd wander around the settlement a little, on my own. See what the place was like at night, without Rojas to interpret it for me.

I headed down the path toward the plaza, surrounded by dense black shadows relieved here and there by the thick yellow light of kerosene lamps shining out of open doors and windows. I nodded and smiled at the carpenter as I passed, and he did the same. I said *buenas noches* to the four or five shadowy figures I met, and they replied. Most even smiled. When I reached the plaza I stopped and looked up at the stars. Wreck Bay really was one of those towns where they roll up the sidewalks at night. Or would if there were any sidewalks. I walked over to naval headquarters. The sentry, who was leaning tiredly against the gatepost, nodded as I walked in. The sailor at the reception desk glanced up, then went back to reading a paperback book. I returned to the plaza and studied the stars again.

Becker, Thompson, and López. They were connected. I had to know more about all of them. I'd already started on the German and the American. Now I had to start on my boss, the man who held my life in his hands. Investigating your boss when you're the ultimate outsider could be very dangerous. Fatal. But it had to be done and I might as well get started. I walked back through the shadows to the Miramar and arrived just in time to see López storming out of the entrance, shouting at García, the owner. I stopped in the shadows. I had no idea what they were arguing about, but I could see that both were angry. García returned to his restaurant, and another shadow moved toward López, who was standing next to his motorcycle. The shadow moved into the light, and I saw that it was Esme, the young prostitute the sergeant had shooed away shortly after I first arrived at Wreck Bay. López shouted at her then held out his hand. Esme put something into it. Money, I assumed. Then she disappeared into the night. López jumped onto his bike, kick-started it, and growled down the sandy road.

I returned to *Pegasus* and lay down in the cockpit, looking up at the stars. Light and dark, I thought. The brilliant, golden noonday sun; the sparkling Pacific; the sensual beauty of the highlands. Ana de Guzmán. And on the other hand: López, the governor, three murders, hatreds carried all the way from the Old World. I dragged myself below and spent a sleepless night trying to concentrate on the prospect of seeing Ana again and not thinking about the new danger I was putting myself into by nosing around López's life.

When my wind-up alarm clock clanged the next morning—I did finally fall asleep at some point—I woke up still thinking about Ana. I dressed quickly and, while the new day was little more than a golden glow along the eastern horizon, rowed in to the dock. I reached the gunboat in time to share some rice, beans, and fruit with the crew, and then we were underway. All the while, Ana was still on my mind, and there she remained until we passed Isla del Torre, about halfway to Santa Cruz. This bleak, lonely pile of igneous rock, composed almost entirely of a towering spire of jet-black volcanic stone, is a stunning sight, one brought to life by the massive flocks of black-and-orange frigate birds that nest on its dark cliffs, wheeling and screaming at the seagulls that try to share the air with them. As I watched the birds, a local fishing boat passed into view from behind the tower, sailing in the steady breeze toward Wreck Bay. I borrowed the skipper's binoculars and thought I recognized Gregor. "Ask the skipper to go alongside that fishing boat," I said to Rojas.

It *was* Gregor. He was seated on a box with his arm lying across the tiller, wearing a floppy straw hat. He seemed half asleep. As the gunboat slowed alongside the fishing boat, I leaned over and shouted, "Gregor! That was a great party the other night."

"Wasn't it?" he shouted back without moving, a big grin on his face. "Are you on your way to steal my wife or visit Ana?"

"I thought I'd try both."

"You're a braver man than I."

"Aren't you far from home?"

"The fish make me work. I have to chase them all over the ocean, wherever they decide to go." He then laughed and waved; I waved back, and we each continued on to our destinations.

We arrived at Santa Cruz early in the afternoon to find Ana, Don Vicente, and his wife standing on the long stone pier. Parked at the foot of the dock was Don Vicente's large, shiny Ford convertible. His launch was moored to the far side. Our hosts were surrounded by two dozen of the island's other inhabitants. Some, I learned later, were Don Vicente's employees; others were settlers. Any visit, by anybody, was something of an event in the Galápagos.

"Welcome, Fred, I'm so glad you came," said Ana, practically gushing, as I stepped ashore. Her smile was brilliant and happy but far from serene. Buried somewhere within it was tension and even a little fear. It worried me, and I hoped she would reveal the cause before any of those fears came true.

"Fred, my friend," said Don Vicente, stepping forward and grabbing my hand before Ana could hug me or commit some other such impropriety in front of the crowd. "May I present my wife, Doña María," he continued, guiding me toward a very attractive middle-aged woman who looked exactly as I imagined Ana would in another twenty years.

"Welcome, Fred," said Doña María in English. She spoke with a fascinating mixture of dignity coupled with an almost mischievous grin. What a family, I thought. Three coconspirators. "Vicente and Ana have said so many nice and interesting things about you."

I smiled and took her hand, wondering exactly what she meant—or maybe what she felt—about the "interesting things."

"And this is Seaman Rojas," chimed in Ana, nodding toward my assistant.

"Welcome, Seaman," said Doña María, bestowing a smile on the young sailor. "I've also heard about your part in Fred's adventures."

"Nothing embarrassing, I hope, Doña."

"Not to my mind."

"Come along," said Don Vicente, striding through the casual, loosely packed crowd, chatting with many people as he progressed toward the convertible. When he reached the side of the car, Ana's father held out his hand for my bag, which he tossed into the trunk. He then held the door for Ana and her mother to climb into the rear seat and for me to settle into the front. Rojas was delegated to the rumble seat between the rear seat and the trunk. "There's so much I want to show you, Fred," shouted my host gleefully as he toured down the gravel road that led from the quay into the scrub.

For the most part, the twisty, at times dusty trip up from the hot coastal area into the more temperate zone was familiar. Thanks to my hosts, however, I did learn the names of dozens of trees and shrubs, some of which I'd already learned to hate. Once we reached the highlands I was thrust into a totally new world.

We popped out of the forest onto a great, green plain, many times larger than that enjoyed by Olaf and Paquita Hanson. The air was cool, and the wind carried the smells of the forest and other growing things. At one end sat a large, two-story stone-and-stucco house with brilliant red terra-cotta roof tiles. At the other end, a dormant volcano, its peak partially shrouded in mist, towered over all. And in between were what must have been fifty acres, all under cultivation of some sort, along with another fifty of pastures, each fenced and containing small herds of different animals—cattle, sheep, horses, goats. For an almost middle-aged New York cop who'd spent ninety-nine percent of his life in a city where only asphalt and bricks ever seemed to take root, the sight was as overwhelming as it was foreign.

Grinning from ear to ear with pride, Don Vicente roared up to the front steps of his house and braked. Roberto appeared on the veranda, walked down the steps, and opened my door. While I slithered out, followed by Ana and Doña María, Don Vicente let himself out and hurried around to the steps. "Come, Fred, you must see our view."

I followed him and gasped as I looked out over dozens of small fields each containing a different crop—pineapples, corn, beans, and I had no idea what else—all surrounded by the lush, green forest.

"Now follow me," he insisted. We walked around the veranda to a side of the house I'd not seen from the driveway. There was a small swimming pool surrounded by an inviting shaded patio. But that wasn't the attraction. From where I stood I could see, in almost all directions, the Pacific in all its choppy, blue-and-white glory.

"This is magnificent, sir," I gasped. The house itself was impressive by any standards, except perhaps those of the Rockefellers, but it was the view that took my breath away.

"Let me show you to your room, then we'll eat. After lunch Ana can give you a tour while I take a brief rest. Do you ride?"

"Horses?"

"Yes."

"Not well."

"She'll use the car, then."

Don Vicente led me up to my second-floor room, where my seabag had already been delivered. The room, like the rest of the house, had a light, open feel. The furniture looked expensive, but it lacked the dark, heavy feel of the baroness's bedroom, and the walls were enlivened with art that was cheerful and bright, except for the brooding portraits in darkened and cracked oil of a few long-gone relatives. After my brief tour, we returned to a small alcove set in the veranda next to the pool. There, Ana and Doña María were already seated at a table, chatting comfortably. "What do you think of the view, Fred?" asked Ana.

"Wonderful. And I really mean it."

"Now you see why I like it so much here," she replied.

Don Vicente and I sat, and the meal—lamb, rice, beans, and a salad—arrived almost immediately. "Have you lived in New York all your life?" asked Doña María.

"Yes."

"And Ana tells us you're an orphan," she continued, as a yellow-and-red butterfly drifted past and landed lightly on the railing along one side of the patio.

"Yes, most of my family died from influenza in 1918."

"I'm sorry. So many died everywhere. Including my brother, Rafael. You're a policeman?"

As she said it, the faintest hint of disapproval crept into Doña María's voice. I had to keep reminding myself that I was surrounded by hundreds of years of wealth and power—wealth and power that would find a common policeman far from impressive. Even I was surprised by Ana's fascination with me. "I used to be. Then I decided the world is bigger than the streets of Manhattan."

"María," said Don Vicente, chuckling as he leaned toward his wife, "you're being a little snobby. You enjoy socializing with the Herzogs, Gregor and Carla. And the Echeverrías. Whatever Fred may have been, and I'm sure he was not only an honest and skilled police officer but also one destined for advancement, he's now an adventurer like the rest of us. And a very presentable young man. We're not in Quito, where your friend Elvira Torres, or certain of our cousins, can huff and puff about my follies or the sort of people we associate with."

Doña María seemed to look inside herself a moment, then burst into a slightly rueful smile. "Pardon me, Fred," she said,

"Vicente is quite right. I'm being foolish. Old habits die hard. I lived for almost a year in New York and know perfectly well Quito isn't the center of the universe. As for the Herzogs, they're very entertaining, although a little roguish. Especially Gregor."

"You're not having second thoughts about sending me to Barnard, are you?" asked Ana.

"Of course not. We're both very pleased with what you learned there. About biology and about life."

"Do you miss Quito when you're here?" I asked, then worried that I'd spoken out of place.

"A little, at times," laughed Doña María in an almost convincing way. "We spend about six months here every year. Vicente often spends another one or two without me. If this were a normal country home, I might be bored, but I become very involved in some of Vicente's experiments. That's one of the main reasons I married him, because his tinkering seemed more interesting than the endless sessions of riding, shooting, playing cards, and drinking that the other young men devoted themselves to. I'm very proud of him, really. He's managed to discover several techniques that other farmers seem to find very useful."

Based on that revelation, I concluded that Doña María was prepared to tolerate me. At least as long as we were in Las Encantadas.

While Don Vicente and his wife disappeared for a short siesta, a nap dictated more by habit than need since the weather remained bracing, Roberto brought the Ford around. "Bring your revolver," directed Ana, the edge of tension now evident in her voice. "We'll probably see wild pigs. The whale ships brought them, along with the goats and rats, more than 150 years ago. They turned wild and now tear up the planted fields whenever they get a little hungry."

I suspected that the pigs weren't the only reason she wanted me armed, but I already knew her well enough to know that she wouldn't like being pushed. I simply had to trust her judgment. I returned to my room for the revolver. As I trotted down the veranda steps to the car, Roberto was asking Ana something. Ana, who was dressed for the expedition in a bush jacket and baggy pants, shook her head and smiled. She glanced at my revolver, hurried back into the house a moment, and returned with a shotgun, which she laid in the back seat.

"Will that stop a wild pig?"

"It will with these," she replied, holding up a box of solid shot.

"What about Rojas?" I asked as Ana started the big car, put it in gear, and headed down the driveway. "I haven't seen him since Roberto dragged him off before lunch to talk about boats."

"I think Papa wants to show him his citrus tree grafts. He thinks Rojas will become somebody once he gets out of the navy. Otherwise he can amuse himself in the pool."

She paused a moment as she concentrated on driving. "It's good you told Papa you don't feel comfortable riding. Now we'll have to walk a little, but if we were on horseback and something went wrong . . ."

"What could go wrong? We're going on a tour of your father's experiments, aren't we? Are wild pigs really that dangerous?"

"In part," she said as she tooled down a dirt road between two fields, one planted with corn and one with cabbages. Standing in the middle of the cabbages were two field hands.

They waved us over. Ana stopped. "I'll be right back." She climbed out of the car and walked over to the hands. After studying the plants a minute or two, they all started laughing. It looked as if they were congratulating each other. Ana then waved at them and returned to the car. "Look carefully at those cabbages. Some are bigger than others, no?"

"Yes."

"That's because Papa and I came up with a new fertilizer mixture. We can make them grow faster, and they taste just as good as the original. And the fertilizer is cheap."

Although I was truly interested in the cabbages—I was interested in anything involving Ana—it was time to get down to business. "Why did you send me that strange message?"

Ana put the car back in gear before she replied. "Because your friend Herr Becker is here. About five miles away. I spotted him the day before yesterday. He was hiking around the sides of the volcano, collecting rocks and surveying. When I caught up with him, he was a little surprised but not upset. He has a camp set up and plans to stay a few days, then move on."

"You talked to him?"

"Of course. I told you I've met him before, at Wreck Bay."

"Does Don Vicente know?"

"No. He dislikes Becker and thinks he's very dangerous. I don't want to worry him."

"Why didn't you tell me right away?"

"Because I'm a little worried about it all. But I know we have to see him, to find out if he did kill the baroness and her two lapdogs."

"Did he say what he was doing?"

"It was obvious that he's collecting rock samples. He's a geologist."

"What, exactly, is he looking for?"

"He didn't say, and I didn't push him since he isn't on our land. I do know that all sorts of minerals are associated with volcanoes."

"Whose land is he on?"

"It belongs to the government now. Originally it was part of a big plantation that included our property back in the days of the penal colonies. The man who owned all the land was a brutal fellow who rented prisoners to work for him and abused them terribly. Then one night he just disappeared. When no relatives could be found, the government took the land and sold part to Papa. It still owns the rest, as far as we know, although it's now occupied by a dozen or so squatters."

"Is Becker going to welcome us?"

"I think he'll be happy to see me again."

I wondered if he'd even remember me.

19

We continued down the road through the center of Don Vicente's plantation, past an astounding variety of plants—everything from asparagus to garbanzo beans to artichokes. On the right a hill appeared. It was covered with vines on wires. "Grapes?" I asked.

"Yes. I think they're delicious, but Papa's very disappointed with the wine he's managed to make from them. See that low building over there? That's his winery."

"I'd like to see it some day."

"Maybe tomorrow. You can try some of the product. I don't think it's that bad. We'll also go to the greenhouse so I can show you some of my experiments on flowers."

I leaned back in the seat and tried to relax. Ana, the day, the gentle breeze filled with the good smells of growing things, the green forest and fields and the blue sky. The absence of López.

I tried desperately to relax but couldn't. Instead, I found myself trapped between two armies warring in my mind. My God, how I wanted to be part of all that surrounded me. To be with Ana, to hear her, to feel her, to help her grow the biggest damn cabbages in the entire universe. That was the army I wanted to join, but at the moment that army was only a dream. The other army marched under the flag of reality, and it was much closer, much more immediate. López, the baroness's murderer, prison, and very possibly a miserable death. And closest of all was Becker. He was probably armed, he had a temper, and I felt certain he was a pretty tough fellow. Ana was obviously nervous, and she knew him better than I did. I hoped that we'd meet and chat and I'd get a feel for him and what he was doing. And what he might know about the baroness. I hoped everything would go smoothly, but hopes are very much like dreams. You can't count on them.

"Hang on," Ana said as she turned off the gravel road onto a much narrower and rougher track that led into the surrounding forest. She continued to slow, and the car shuddered and rolled as we wound our way forward and then up the sides of the green-dressed volcano.

"Isn't this hard on the car?"

"If we break it Papa will just order parts and fix it. In the meantime he'll make do with horses." By this time we were creeping through stands of evergreens and oaks. As the track narrowed to a footpath, Ana braked the car. "This is it. From here on we do a little work."

"How far is his camp?"

"About a mile."

We put the top up on the car, showers being frequent in the highlands, especially around the mountains. Ana grabbed her shotgun. "Every time I've seen him Becker has been civil, even enthusiastic, but no matter how he acts I can always feel a powerful sense of arrogance and anger. It shows in his eyes. There's something not quite right about him."

"That's the impression I got," I said as I checked the load in my revolver. "Everyone says he has a very bad temper. Was he armed when you last saw him?"

"Yes, a pistol. And several of the hands have heard what they thought were gunshots coming from there the past few days."

"OK, we've got to act friendly. Remember that we have these"—I pointed to our weapons—"because we're hunting pigs. At the same time we can't forget that there's a chance this guy's a very brutal murderer. Of three people."

"OK, Sheriff, I've got it. And if he can't come up with the right answers are you going to arrest him?" She tried to sound light.

"No. I want to talk to him. Size him up. He can't go anywhere until the next Guayaquil boat."

With Ana leading, we moved up the path, alert for ambush and saying little. I wondered briefly if I should have brought Rojas along but decided there was little he could contribute, although I assumed he knew how to handle a gun.

The hike didn't prove to be overly long, but it did prove challenging, since much of it was almost straight up. We were both huffing when we reached a small clearing on one of the overgrown ridges that stretched out from the volcano. "Somebody was obviously here," I remarked as I looked down at the scuffed and trampled ground.

"Damn," mumbled Ana under her breath as she walked over to one side of the clearing. "We just missed him."

I joined her and found myself looking out over the Pacific, only a couple hundred yards away but hundreds of feet below. I wondered how the German had managed to carry all his gear down the steep trail that led to the small beach below us. A fisherman's sailboat was clearly visible, headed west. And a launch was also there, fast disappearing to the south.

Damn fast! In fact it wasn't a launch, it was a speedboat. "Who does that boat belong to?" I asked.

"I don't know," said Ana, peering hard at it. "Fast, isn't it? The Castros were talking about getting one, but I don't think they have yet. They live on San Cristóbal."

"What about López? I hear he has his own boat at the governor's mansion."

She paused to look again at the fast-disappearing craft. "You're right. It might be his. I've seen it before, but I can't be sure at this distance."

"Why the hell would he be here?"

Ana just shrugged. "I'm sorry. I was sure I could deliver this guy to you." To be honest, she sounded a little relieved.

"You got me closer than I've managed to get on my own," I replied as I stared out at our escaping quarry. The sailboat, I figured, must belong to Pepe Hernández, the fisherman Piers Hanson said was chauffeuring Becker around, and the speedboat had to be López. But why was the sergeant here? It had been obvious that Becker and López didn't like each other.

"Fred, look at these."

I turned but Ana was gone. "Where are you?"

"Back here."

I followed her voice and spotted the indentation in an outcrop of dark volcanic rock. I walked into the shallow cave and found Ana on her hands and knees in the middle, scooping up some gray, metallic-looking stones. "Those look like the rocks I saw in the baroness's living room," I remarked, "the ones that disappeared while I was trapped in the cellar. Any idea what they are?"

"Some sort of ore. When we get back to the house I can look in Papa's books—he has thousands of them. Whatever they are, they do prove Becker's a geologist."

"Yes, but why was he visiting the baroness just before she was murdered?"

"Why did everybody visit the baroness?"

"And what's his connection with López? The one time I met him, he didn't seem to like the sergeant."

"Undoubtedly political in some way."

From the tone of her voice, she was more interested in the rocks than in López. Whether the connection was political or criminal, it was now clear that it existed and that it explained, in some way, López's determination to hide Becker from me.

While Ana continued collecting ore samples, I backed out of the cave and walked around the clearing again, looking at the ground and listening to the birds carry on in the trees. After finding nothing of interest, I wandered along the face of the dark outcrop that rose from one side of the open space. There was, I realized, an even darker area on the cliff face, partially hidden by a tangled, light-green shrub. I forced my way through its branches and discovered another cave. Although it was deeper than the first, it wasn't too deep for the green, tree-filtered sunlight to penetrate. I eased myself in and immediately tripped over a small circle outlined by stones. Within the circle, ashes were still discernible, along with what looked like fish bones. I continued my search and found little else of interest except a name, ORTEGA, scratched faintly on one wall. Who was Ortega? A hunter or fisherman or perhaps a prisoner from the old penal colony? I wondered if somebody had lived here for any length of time, or if Ortega had just been a casual visitor.

Light and dark. The phrase popped into my head again.

I wandered back across the clearing toward the opening that looked out over the ocean. Something on the ground glinted. I reached down for it. It was a shell casing from a pistol. And there were several more spread around in a small area. All fresh-looking. I wondered what my quarry had been shooting at. Probably frigate birds and seagulls.

Having missed Becker, my first impulse was to get right back to the house and call for the gunboat to pick me up as soon as possible. I thought about it and knew that would undoubtedly be a mistake. It would tell López that I was, despite his orders, still chasing Becker rather than wooing Ana. Even more dangerous, it might tell him that I knew he was somehow involved with the elusive German. "Let's go pig hunting," I suggested. "We can look in your father's books later."

After dinner that night, Ana disappeared into her father's study. A few minutes later I followed. And Don Vicente followed me.

Ana looked up from an opened book. Beside it were the rock samples she'd picked up at Becker's camp.

We both smiled.

"This one," she said, pointing at a sample that looked like a dull piece of metal, "looks like wolframite. And these," she added, pointing at some crystals that looked as if they'd been coated with oil, "could be scheelite. Both are ores of tungsten."

"Indeed," said Don Vicente, "tungsten. Everybody, the Germans, the British, the Americans, are desperate to get more of it. They use it to make steel very hard. To make cutting tools and armor. Where did you find them?"

Ana looked up at her father, more than a hint of guilt in her eyes. "The German, Becker, had a camp on the side of the volcano for the past few days. We dropped by so Fred could meet him, but he'd already left."

Don Vicente looked at her a moment in silence. Then at me. I'm certain he was asking himself why he hadn't left Ana with the nuns a little longer. "Just what we might expect to find in a German geologist's camp," he remarked with a sigh.

I had as much of an answer for the commandant as I was ever likely to have, but I still didn't know who killed the baroness, which meant I still had to find Becker. The impulse to call for the gunboat to pick me up the next day was almost overpowering. "When's the next Guayaquil boat due?" I asked Don Vicente.

"In a few days, almost a week. You still have time."

Ana seemed to realize that whatever her father thought, I didn't think I had much time. Her face spoke of both worry and disappointment. I knew I should go, but I didn't want to. I thought of the brilliant blue Pacific and the cool breezes and Ana. There was a good chance that once I left Santa Cruz I'd never enjoy any of them again, thanks to López. Since everybody thought I was on a short vacation, I might as well continue the deception. I'd still have time to find Becker.

In the end, Rojas and I spent two more very happy days at Don Vicente's personal resort and playground. We admired his projects, many of which involved either improving certain crops or getting them to grow where they don't normally. I learned the most astounding things, like how to get one citrus tree to grow lemons, limes, grapefruits, and two different kinds of oranges, each on a separate branch. I tried my hand at tennis and played bridge for the first time. I received two riding lessons and learned that Rojas already knew a great deal about horses. The wild pigs proved too wily for us, so we soothed our bruised egos by playing in the pool. All the while I basked in the glow of Ana's smiles.

During that whole time, after I made the decision to stay, I managed to keep the baroness, Becker, and López banished to the distant edge of my thoughts. With one exception. Not having yet mastered the art of the siesta, I was sitting on the patio after lunch on the second day, staring at the photos I'd found in the baroness's room. Ana appeared and settled beside me. "Why aren't you napping?" I asked.

"I seem to have lost the habit. I must have been in New York too long. What are those?"

I showed her the photos and told her where I'd found them.

"*Dios mío,*" she said after leafing through them. "I feel like I know this woman now. If things had gone differently in Quito, I could have turned out like her."

I looked at her, waiting.

"She was a happy kid, and then something bad happened to her family and she ended up with this pig in the Nazi uniform. Look at how she shoved a pencil or something through his face. God, how she must have hated him. And then she kept the picture to remind herself of her hatred."

"You couldn't be like her. You don't hate anybody."

"I don't usually, except maybe López, but I can. Fred, we have to find who killed her!"

"Yes, we do." For more than one reason, I added to myself.

The third and last morning, I woke up at dawn and walked out to the veranda, next to the pool. The blue-gray world was very quiet, the night mist that nourished all of Don Vicente's experiments still dissolving. I thought of Héctor Echeverría's words that things were happening in Las Encantadas. He was right—exciting things were happening here, even on the edge of the world. New people were settling, new languages were arriving along with new traditions and, if Echeverría and Don Vicente were successful, new agricultural practices. But things were happening everywhere. And many of the changes were far from positive. In Europe, armies were already marching.

I wanted to be part of the new life here, where I could see much further than I'd ever been able to see in Hell's Kitchen. I could sign on with Don Vicente and have Ana at my side. I took a deep breath, and my dreams disintegrated. I couldn't settle here. The NYPD and the Mob would eventually find me. I'd had my fun. Now I had to escape López and after that, God only knew.

Whatever remained of my fantasies ended abruptly later that morning when the gunboat pulled alongside the pier. I was standing with the de Guzmáns, deciding whether to peck Ana on the cheek or to go for broke and really kiss her, when I noticed the expression on the skipper's face. Catastrophe had somehow struck while I wasn't looking. Even before the lines had been passed ashore, the petty officer was shouting at Rojas. I was surrounded by shocked gasps. Rojas, Ana, Doña María, and Don Vicente, everybody knew except me. Even the half-dozen idlers lounging around on the pier looked shocked.

"There's been a terrible disaster, sir," explained Rojas. "Last night your boat caught fire and sank."

I just stared at him a moment, my shock even greater than that of those around me. *Pegasus*, my boat, burned and sunk! Everything I owned gone. I was trapped forever. And she wasn't even my boat, I reminded myself as a wave of gut-wrenching guilt exploded within me. *Pegasus* was Alf's boat. I'd stolen her from him and now I'd destroyed her. That remorse I'd held in check so long now threatened to overwhelm me. I realized I was shuddering slightly.

"Fred, are you all right?" asked Ana as she grabbed my arm.

I turned to her and looked into her eyes. All I could see was concern. Not a hint of accusation. But then she knew nothing of this, my worst sin. "I'll be all right, Ana. It's just the shock. I'd better get back right away."

Don Vicente stepped beside me and grabbed my arm with one hand while he pumped my hand with the other. "It will work out, my friend. Do what you must, and let me know if there's anything I can do. And remember, you're always welcome to come visit again and to stay as long as you want."

Under other circumstances those words would have seemed heaven-sent.

I thanked him and shook Doña María's hand. On her face was a worried little smile. Then Ana grabbed me and hugged me tight. "We're all on your side, Fred." I pecked her on the cheek and jumped aboard the gunboat, closely followed by Rojas. The gunboat's engine backed with a roar and a cloud of black smoke, and we pulled away from the dock.

As soon as we were clear of the bay, the skipper came aft to where we were standing. He nodded to me with a sympathetic expression, then started talking to Rojas. "It seems, sir," reported my aide and translator, "that a fire broke out very late last night. Nobody knows how it started. The commandant sent men to put it out, but they weren't able to do so. The boat was wood, and no longer young."

"And now?"

"What's left of her is sitting on the bottom of Wreck Bay."

The words were brutal, but how else could he have put it? Alf's boat was gone, and my future was growing darker by the second.

It probably would have been better if *Pegasus* had been lost far at sea, in deep water. Then she would have disappeared and been gone. Only a memory. But she'd sunk in Wreck Bay, so as we passed her resting place, the top three or four feet of her mainmast were sticking out of the water. A very painful reminder. "I want to dive and take one last look at her," I remarked to Rojas. "I probably can't get all the way down, but I can at least see how she looks now."

"I'm sure we can find a mask for you, sir."

Rojas's friend Gonzales was standing on the dock, waiting for us. "Sir," he announced in slow and careful English, as if he'd memorized it, "the commandant wishes to see you right now. Please come with me."

"Yes, of course." I turned to Rojas. "I think your friend is trying to take your job away from you."

"He won't be in the navy forever, sir."

I wasn't sure what to expect, but the interview with the commandant was brief and relatively painless. "Mr. Freiman," he said in his own slow English, "I am very sorry you have lost your yacht. I also very much regret that we were unable to save it."

"Thank you, sir. I know you did your best."

He nodded, then continued, "As I am sure you understand, I will have to cut off the masts. Both of them. They are very dangerous navigational hazards."

"I totally agree, sir. Would there be any objection to my diving down as close as I can get to take one last look?"

"No, not at all. Where do you plan to live?"

Good question. "I don't know at the moment."

"I can provide a room here, or perhaps you can find something else." As he spoke, he handed me a wad of sucres.

"Thank you. I'll come up with something."

He started to rise, and so did I. "Have you learned anything more about how the fire started, sir?"

He raised his eyebrows. "No. That is something of a mystery. Most boat fires I have seen are either from an electrical short circuit or somebody being careless smoking or cooking.

Neither would seem to apply here. When I send the diver
down to cut the masts, I will have him look carefully around.
He is not a trained investigator, but he is an experienced seaman and may spot something."

"If you do find something, will you please let me know?"

"With pleasure."

Rojas was waiting for me outside the commandant's office.
"Where to now, sir?"

Yes, where to now? "Do you have any idea where López
is?"

"No, sir. Nobody's seen him."

I looked up at the sun. There was still plenty of daylight
left. "You said you could get me a dive mask. Can you also
get me a boat so we can go out and take a look at what's
left of *Pegasus*?"

"Of course, sir."

An hour later Rojas was rowing me out across the deep
blue bay. I secured the boat's painter to *Pegasus*'s masthead
and only then noticed a small, splotchy black-and-white something perched on the tilted mast, right at the waterline. While
the boat drifted back on its ten-foot painter, Rojas started to
smile, then stifled it, realizing that now clearly wasn't the
time for chuckles. Ignoring this unexplained mirth, I slipped
the mask over my face. "Keep your eyes open for sharks," I
directed. He grabbed the oar and shook it.

I lowered myself over the side of the rowboat and breast-
stroked slowly to the mast. Alf's boat was under about forty
feet of water, which meant I could probably get down to it
but would have no breath left for much exploring. Still, I
had to take one last look. To see if there was anything to see.

As I got closer, I took another look at the black-and-white
blob on the mast. It was rocking slowly from foot to foot. It

was a tiny penguin—a Galápagos penguin, as I later learned—
no more than nine inches high, and whoever had decorated it
must have been drunk, because the black and white areas were
ill-defined, almost random. It had preposterous little wings,
a back straight enough to satisfy the most demanding marine
drill sergeant, and a long beak. More than happy to hunt for
little fish in the chill waters of the Humboldt Current.

I continued to approach the mast, not as interested in the
bird as Rojas seemed to be. The little penguin watched me,
turning its head from side to side to give each beady little
eye a chance to study me. Suddenly it sprang backward into
the water, flipped its bottom skyward, did a surface dive,
and was gone.

Holding my breath, I looked down. Thanks to the crystal
clarity of the water, I was rewarded with a distant, shadowy
sight of the boat. *Rewarded* isn't the correct word in this
case. Even from the distance, I could see that much of the
cabin had disappeared along with a big chunk of the side. I
raised my head again and, holding on to the mast, took several deep breaths. I grabbed one of the wire stays that still
held the mast up and pulled myself down on it. The deeper I
went, the chillier the water became and the more the pressure
increased on my chest and ears, but I did manage to make it
all the way to the deck.

Close up, *Pegasus* was a worse mess than it had appeared
from the surface. Half the cabin was gone, with only a few
charred lengths of lumber to show where it had been. A
great black void stretched down the side from the deck to
the waterline. Despite the growing agony in my lungs, I stuck
my head into what had been the cabin and saw nothing but
darkness. That was it! I'd seen what there was to see, and
now I had to concentrate on saving myself. With my lungs

engulfed in flames, I sprang off the deck and headed for the surface, hoping I would make it before my will weakened and I gulped in a deadly dose of water.

As I approached the surface I detected motion, rapid motion, off to one side. God! I thought. The sharks have finally arrived. I kicked and pulled my arms down to accelerate my ascent, then watched in surprise and relief as the little penguin raced past me, feet kicking furiously.

Somehow I made it. My head broke through the surface, and I gulped frantically for air. By my second breath I found the wits to grab the mast and float, gasping and shaking. Whether the swimming bird was chasing a fish or just taking another look at me I'll never know.

"I'm here, sir."

I looked up and found Rojas in the boat only a few feet away. "I can haul you in, sir."

"In a minute. I've got to catch my breath."

God damn López! He'd killed *Pegasus*, killed Alf's dream, and killed my future. Not to mention my self-respect.

20

I opened my eyes because I had no choice; the sun pouring in through the window had pried them open for me. My head pounded as I looked around the room, and reality took a minute to register. I wasn't aboard *Pegasus*. I was lying in the simple but fairly clean shack Rojas had helped me find behind the very modest home of Wreck Bay's only tailor. A bed, a small table with one chair, a window, a beaten earth floor, and a privy out back. I lay there, wrapped in misery and cursing myself for spending the night guzzling first beer and then rum. Most of all, I cursed myself for stealing Alf's boat and then losing it.

I told myself that just as soon as I felt a little better I'd hunt down that bastard López and kill him, but even in my half-dead mental condition I knew I wouldn't. No matter how much the commandant might sympathize with such an act, he'd have no choice but to arrest me and send me to the mainland for killing a government official. There was a knock at the door. I tried to focus on what looked like a large cockroach strolling along the wall—a big, New York roach—

and hoped whoever wanted to visit would go away. A second knock. Then "Fred, it's Ana. Can I come in?"

Ana, I thought. Yes, Ana. A spark of hope and joy ignited in my soul only to flutter and sputter pitifully under the weight of my hangover. I wanted to see her, but I didn't want her to see me the way I was. I mumbled something, and the door opened. Ana walked in, followed by Roberto. In her arms was a large package wrapped in paper. She put it on the table and pulled the chair next to the bed. "I'm so sorry about your boat, Fred. I'd really hoped that when this was over we might go adventuring in it," she said, touching me gently on the cheek. "They said you made a mess of yourself last night."

I damn well did, I thought as I stared at the ceiling. And I made an ass of myself, too. I looked at her and tried to focus, finally succeeding. "I've got to clean myself up a little." Roberto, I noticed, was wearing a faint but seemingly sympathetic smile. Maybe he was defrosting a little.

"Yes, you do, but first I want you to try these on," she said, pointing at the package. "They're old but still presentable. Papa's taller than you, so we altered them. They should fit. I'll go outside while Roberto helps you." She turned and glided out the door.

I struggled to stand and realized there was something I had to do before trying on clothes. I pointed to the back door, and Roberto nodded. Without bothering to put on my worthless canvas shoes, I shuffled out the door and across the sandy, stony backyard past a tiny, compost-based vegetable garden. After visiting the privy, which I understood was flushed out naturally by every high tide, I scooped some water from a barrel of freshwater and threw it on my face. The water didn't make me feel much better, but I thought I could make it through the fitting. When I got back into the room, I found three pairs of vary serviceable cotton trousers, three or four shirts, some undergarments that looked new, a pair of swim shorts, and a pair of leather sandals all laid out on the bed. Without a mirror and with half my brain still shattered, I had no way of knowing how well the clothes fit, but Roberto nodded his approval in every case. The last thing I tried was the swim shorts, which I left on. Roberto glanced at me, then stuck his head out the door, and Ana glided back into the room. "Well?"

"They're very handsome and fit perfectly," I tried to assure her. "Don Vicente keeps doing me favors I can't repay."

"Favors? You mean old clothes? Well, the truth is he isn't much of a clothes hog. The things he wears out here are usually even worse than what he's sent you. Mama doesn't let him get away with that on the mainland."

I looked again at the clothes and decided I was going to be better dressed than ninety percent of the Galapaguinos.

"Ana, if I'm ever going to return to the living I have to take a swim."

"Before you go, sit down and chew on this a few minutes." She handed me a piece of paper folded over into a small package. I opened it and found ground-up leaves sprinkled with a white powder. I looked at her, then stuffed the mess in my mouth and chewed. Within seconds I found my lips puckering. "What's this?"

"Coca leaves, a mild narcotic. It'll help you feel better."

"What? The stuff they make cocaine out of?" I thought of all the cocaine in the streets of Hell's Kitchen. They said it made life bearable, like alcohol.

"Yes. But this is much milder. And legal. Think of it as a super aspirin."

I looked at her skeptically but started to chew. Anything to quell the civil war in my head. After a few minutes I felt better . . . and more alive. "I could get to like this stuff," I mumbled.

"Over my dead body. The only people who use it regularly are the Indians in the high mountains. It helps them survive, but it's not good for them. I'm only giving you this because it's an emergency."

"Have you ever used it?"

"Twice. Once when I was little and broke my arm falling off a horse. The doctor was hours away and I was making a terrible racket, so Papa gave me some coca tea. How do you feel now?"

"Better. Much better."

"Spit it out," she demanded. "Here, in this bag. Now take your swim. Roberto and I will go along and guard against the sharks."

The sharp tone of Ana's voice surprised me, but it shouldn't have. I was the one who'd made a fool out of himself, and she was putting me back together. I was going to have to do some of the work myself!

I don't know if it was the coca or the swim, but within an hour I felt as if I could pay attention to the world around me rather than blundering around in the chaos inside my head. Now I could focus on the business at hand. "What I'd really like to do is shoot López," I said as I chewed some rice and beans while we sat in a little hole-in-the-wall, two-table restaurant owned and operated by a friend of Roberto's. "Or plant an ax in his head, slowly. But that would really be stupid."

"Yes, it would. I think we've got to concentrate on finding who killed the baroness and her friends. And make absolutely sure that Becker isn't just spreading rock samples around to confuse us. If we can satisfy both López and the commandant, you might get out of this mess alive."

Except for the Mob, of course, and certain influential and highly respected members of the NYPD. There was only one way they'd be satisfied. And I *had* noticed the "we" but prudently let it pass, because despite my initial fear of putting her in danger, I was becoming very comfortable working with her.

"Here's what we have," I said after taking another gulp of coffee. "Just about everybody who knew her disliked her, and all seem capable of killing her and her friends. However, so far I've only found four people who can be placed at the castle during those two days—Thompson, Becker, Elías, and Sofía. Thompson and Elías admit they were there, and Elías says Becker was also there; I think the rock specimens confirm that."

"Unless they were Thompson's. He seems to be collecting rocks, or something, too."

"That's possible. But he seems to have disliked her less than most of the others."

"You overlooked López and yourself. And Ritter and Ernst."

"Yes, I did. And speaking of López, I did tell you the rocks disappeared between when they threw me in the hole and when they dragged me out again. I wonder who took them."

"The maid, Sofía, may have cleaned them up. Or Ritter and Ernst may have taken them."

"Why?"

"Because they resented whoever left them? They were both very strange."

"Or López. He *did* have a briefcase with him."

"Why? Evidence?"

"That makes sense. And if that was López's boat we saw at Becker's camp, then he's more closely connected with Becker than he's admitting."

I paused a moment. "We keep forgetting about Ritter and Ernst. Plenty of people had a reason to kill the baroness, but what about her two pets? They might have done it themselves."

"You think it might have something to do with sex or jealousy? Maybe they were infuriated by her visitors."

"Maybe it was about money. She had all of it, they had none. They probably had to beg for every sucre."

"Then why would somebody kill them?"

"Maybe they didn't kill her. Maybe they saw something."

"Maybe. Fred, why do you think López is so determined for *you* to identify the killer? He knows what he's doing; he could probably do the job himself."

"Don't know. It doesn't make much sense. But I do know we have to pick up where we left off. Find Becker and talk to him, talk to Thompson again, and find Sofía. Somebody has to know where her relatives live."

"I'll ask around about Sofía."

"Thanks. I'll talk to Thompson and get back on Becker's trail." I didn't mention López again because I didn't want her deciding to investigate him herself. Being involved with me was dangerous enough as it was.

"I may still be able to help with Becker. I told you he likes me. He may yet come to me."

I stiffened at the thought. "You mean use you as bait somehow? The man's a shark."

"I've dealt with sharks before." As she said it, there was a tiny gleam in her eye. I already knew that she liked to tiptoe

along the edge; I now realized that if she'd been a man she'd
undoubtedly have taken up bullfighting.

"Do you think Rojas is still alive? He tried to keep up
with me last night," I said as I leaned over to adjust my new
sandals.

"He's tougher than you are. I saw him in the plaza, talking to a girl."

"Well," I replied, not to be outdone by my young naval
assistant, "that's just what I'm doing at the moment, isn't it?"

There was nothing wrong with that little shack I was rent-
ing, but of course it didn't feel like home, like *Pegasus*. After
Ana and Roberto left to head back to Santa Cruz, I decided
to walk down to the beach and do a little more thinking, out
where I could see the world around me. I found my guide
and assistant standing in the plaza, looking out to sea. "How
do you feel, Seaman Rojas?"

He studied me a moment. "Very well, sir," he then replied
with a smile that seemed to confirm his words. Or maybe it
was a slight smirk, since I might still have appeared a little
worse for wear.

We bought a few beers and settled down on the beach
not far from naval headquarters to try again to work it all
out. The breeze, which was stiffening and carried with it the
sharp smells of salt and the black-green seaweed drying on
the beach, drove the remaining cobwebs from my head.

"There, you see them, sir?" said Rojas, breaking a silence
that had temporarily settled over us. As he spoke, he pointed
across the bay.

"What?" I replied, squinting at the opposite shore.

"Seals, sir."

I squinted more vigorously and managed to spot what
looked like four or five swimming dogs. They had the heads

of dogs, but their speed and motion were more like porpoises. "Don't the sharks ever get them?"

"Probably, but I've never seen it in person."

"Everybody in these islands is a fisherman."

We turned at the sound of an engine and watched a big, shiny sedan drive slowly up the path to the stone building and stop. "That's the governor's car," remarked Rojas between sips of beer.

The driver, who was dressed in slacks, a long-sleeved shirt, and real leather shoes, got out, walked over to us, and said something to Rojas. All I understood was *"sargento López."*

"He's been sent to take you to Sergeant López, sir. At his office in the governor's mansion."

The summons was no surprise. "He's using the governor's car now?"

"Why not?"

"He's beginning to act like he's the new governor."

"He's not, but until a new one arrives there's nobody to stop him from using the car. Even the commandant would consider this official business."

It sounded irregular and more than a little threatening to me, but then what choice did I have? I finished off my beer, handed the bottle to Rojas, and followed the driver to the car.

Thanks to the condition of the local roads and the driver's evident desire not to ding or dent the car, the drive out to the mansion, which was several miles up the coast from the settlement, took about half an hour. I looked out at the ocean, then out the other window at the rocks and sand and cactus and the occasional shack set right beside the road. Along the way I had time to think more about my current position and my future and found my anxiety level increasing. In the past, López had always popped out of nowhere to deliver his broadsides, but this time the routine had changed. I'd been summoned and was now being driven off into the falling night, a virtual prisoner. Had I run out of time? I tried the door handle and was relieved to see that it worked. If I got too spooked I could always throw the door open, dive out, and run like hell. But to where? I doubted the driver would even bother to chase me. No matter what happened, the only way I would ever leave Las Encantadas was on the Guayaquil boat. Either as a passenger or as a prisoner.

The governor's mansion vaguely resembled Don Vicente's house—stucco and red tiles—but was considerably larger. It was surrounded by a low wall that seemed of little value other than symbolic. Inside the wall, the grounds were as barren as those without, although Eduardo, the late governor, had clearly made an effort to civilize the bleak scene by placing huge flowerpots filled with blossoms and greenery here and there. Despite his efforts, the mansion appeared a cold and lifeless place, especially in comparison with Don Vicente's. It's possible, though, that the difference wasn't the climate or the gardening or the architecture but rather the presence of Ana.

We parked in the unpaved driveway. Instead of going in through the front entrance, the driver led me around the side of the building. Ahead of me I could see a small inlet with a dock. Tied to that dock was a boat that looked very fast and very familiar. Without stopping, we entered the building through a small door into a corridor that was lined on both sides with heavy wooden doors. I assumed that at least some of these were the colony's civil archives and was proven correct when a door opened and an elderly man came out. Before he closed the door behind him, I saw the room was filled with shelves and boxes, all jammed with papers. The man nodded and turned in the direction from which we'd come. We continued on until we stopped at the last door on the corridor. The driver knocked, then ushered me through into an office.

López stood, hands on hips and wearing his usual gray uniform, looking out a window at the inlet and the launch. "Sit down, Fritz," he said as the driver disappeared through the door. I sat in the chair facing the desk, and López turned and sat in the one behind it. Right there, sitting on the desk, were half a dozen rock samples. They looked just like the ones Ana had found in Becker's camp. And that I'd seen in the baroness's living room.

"You've proven to be a great disappointment, Fritz," he said with an expression of intense, soulless cold. "You keep doing things I tell you not to, and you fail to do what I want you to do."

"Why did you burn *Pegasus*?" I practically snarled, forgetting for a moment my perilous position.

"An unfortunate event for you and also for your uncle. I'm sure there's a lesson to be learned there."

Son of a bitch, I thought. The bastard knows everything! But why not? Alf had undoubtedly reported the boat's disappearance. There was a knock at the door, and the old clerk's head appeared. He said something quickly, and López responded brusquely, "*Bueno*."

"Don't go anywhere, Fritz," he said without a hint of humor as he stepped into the hall.

I stared at the rock samples a moment. There was a well-thumbed book sitting beside them. I looked more closely. It was a DKW motorcycle maintenance manual. I glanced at the door, then stood and leaned over the desk, picking up the manual and opening it. Somebody had been reading it, underlining words and making notes in Spanish. But the manual was in German.

López! The son of a bitch *did* understand German. That pretty much settled it for me. López and Becker were working together. And that was why López wanted Becker cleared of the murder no matter who else had to be railroaded for it. Unfortunately, that still didn't prove that Becker had killed the baroness. Or *why* the sergeant was working with him. Nor did it clear Thompson. I put the manual back where it had been, returned to the chair, and waited.

"Listen carefully, Fritz," said López as he stormed back into the room. "You have three more days to find the murderer and provide me with evidence, totally convincing evidence that will satisfy me, the judge, and the Quito newspapers. If you fail you'll be on the next Guayaquil boat, charged with the three murders here as well as one in New York and stealing a boat. You'll never leave prison alive. And don't think your little señorita and her papa can save you. They may be rich, but they're not as well connected as you may think. Some think the papa is undependable, perhaps not as patriotic as he should be."

As he spoke, López opened the desk drawer and pulled out a pair of rusty and very ugly manacles. "These are from when this was a penal colony," he explained, glowering at me.

I chewed on his threats a moment, then spoke up. "Why do you want me to be the one to identify the murderer?"

"Isn't that obvious? There are many here who don't like me, who don't trust me. If *I* charge somebody there will be doubts. If *you* make the charge and provide the evidence, people will believe, because you're an outsider, an objective outsider."

"And a New York cop?"

"It won't be necessary to mention that, and you probably won't even have to appear in person."

It still made perfect sense. Even more now. López was a German agent, or the agent of a faction in Quito that was pro-German. I considered pushing my luck by telling López we'd seen his boat leaving Becker's camp and asking why he was there. But that would achieve nothing at the moment. He didn't know that I knew he spoke German, and he probably didn't know we'd seen him at Santa Cruz. It was better left that way. For me and for Ana. So I just stared at him.

"Do we understand each other, Fritz? I hope so." He tapped on the cuffs again with his index finger. "Three days, no more. The driver is waiting outside. He'll take you back to the settlement."

When I got back to the beach, I found Rojas sitting right where I'd left him, looking at the whitecaps out in the bay. The seals were still visible. They'd scooted up onto some rocks just off the opposite shore. "Are you all right, sir?"

"Yes," I assured him, though I felt like I'd just been drawn and quartered. "We've got three days to find the killer. Otherwise I'll be on the next Guayaquil boat headed directly for prison."

"I have good news, then. We've located Mr. Thompson. He and his boat are at Baltra Island."

"How'd you find him?"

"We called him on the radio and asked where he was."

21

It wasn't hard to find *Southern Cross*, Thompson's schooner. Baltra is a small island, and while its southern end is dominated by cliffs and an old volcano, its northern end is flat. The boat's two towering masts were visible long before we turned into the island's roundish harbor. As we approached the schooner, I couldn't help but be impressed. It was about sixty feet long and obviously built and equipped for long-distance sailing. It was totally squared away; the brightwork and brass sparkled in the sun, and the canvas awnings glowed. It could have been a warship.

The skipper took the gunboat right alongside the schooner, where we were met by one of the boat's hands—the only person, it turned out, who was aboard.

"Good morning," I shouted.

"Good morning," replied the hand, who was sitting cross-legged on deck, splicing a line. His tone wasn't really friendly, but it wasn't hostile, either.

"Is Mr. Thompson aboard?"

The hand, who wasn't much older than Rojas, squinted at the gunboat a moment and decided he was dealing with authority. "He's ashore, sir, with everybody else." As he spoke he pointed at the flat northern end of the island.

"Thanks," I replied as cheerily as I could. I turned to Rojas. "Ask the skipper to move in closer to that beach and have us rowed ashore. And get some water for us to take along."

Once ashore, there was only one way to go: up and in over the sand and outcrops of sharp volcanic rock. The soles on my newly acquired sandals were infinitely better than those on my canvas shoes, but they provided little protection from sharp pebbles and cacti. I hated to look a gift horse in the mouth, but I did wish Don Vicente had sent some real shoes.

We found Thompson standing at the edge of a large open field decorated with a variety of rocks and stones of all sizes. Beside him, one of his crew was peering through the eyepiece of a surveyor's level. As he watched me approach, a frown appeared on his face. "I assume you have something important to say, Mr. Freiman, since you've chased me all the way out here. Please make it quick; we've got a lot to do today."

"I'll try."

"Is this about the baroness?"

"Yes. You said you visited her within a couple days of her murder. Did you visit her the day she was killed?" I asked, curious if he'd lie about it.

He squinted at me a moment in the bright sunlight. "Yes, although I don't know why I should tell you."

A gust of wind blew a cloud of brown dust around us.

"When?"

"About midmorning."

"And?"

"We socialized."

"Was anybody else there?"

"Her two flunkies, but she sent them away." The guy who was peering through the transit tried to act as if he weren't listening. But, of course, he was.

"Nobody else?"

"I think the maid may have been there at one point. And maybe the cook, but they left."

"Was there anything at all unusual?"

"Not for her. She was in fine form." A brief smile flickered across his face. "She could be very sweet, agreeable, when she wasn't in a rage. I told you she had a temper."

"When did you leave?"

"We got under way shortly after noon. You can check our log or talk to my crew."

"They're *your* crew."

"Any court will accept their oaths."

I looked around. "As a matter of curiosity, what are you doing?"

"Surveying."

"For what?"

"We're thinking about building a new fish cannery here. Tuna. Tuna's hot now, what with the new long-distance tuna clippers."

I glanced at the transit—PROPERTY OF THE UNITED STATES WAR DEPARTMENT. Thompson noted my expression. "Freiman, that's it. I know who you are—you're wanted in New York for murder and the theft of a boat. And you're tied in a little too tight with López. You're not going to ask me any more questions, because I have a lot of work to do and very little time to do it. In fact, you're going to get the hell off this island, right now!"

The shock I felt at Thompson's knowledge was nothing in comparison with that showing on Rojas's face. I knew I'd been bested, and there was no way of getting around it. "OK, Rojas, back to the gunboat." And then, just to maintain a shred of self-respect, I added, "See you around, Thompson."

I explained my sordid past—Sergeant McGrath, that hot evening in Hell's Kitchen, even Erin—to Rojas as we walked back to the beach. By now my feet were totally lacerated despite the sandals' thick soles. It took Rojas a minute or two to digest the sorry saga. "I think you did the right thing to that killer," he concluded. "It's sad you had to leave your friends." As he spoke he looked a little disappointed, almost vexed. I suspect he was unhappy that I hadn't told him the sordid details of my life before. That I hadn't trusted him.

It had been another hot, buggy, frustrating day—one down, two to go—so when we got back to Wreck Bay, I handed Rojas some cash and sent him off for beer. I changed into the swimming shorts Don Vicente had given me and headed down to the beach. Once again, the cool blue water worked its magic, driving away my frustrations, nagging fears, and infuriating bug bites. At least for a few minutes. I was a new man again in a strange new world when I walked out of the Pacific and joined Rojas on the beach.

As I settled into the sand, the seaman popped the top on a bottle and handed it to me. It was almost cold. "The Crazy German is dead," he said with no preamble.

"What?" I demanded. For a few minutes, while I'd been floating in the bay, I'd managed to escape reality. My mind had been filled with Ana and her parents' wonderful planta-tion and impossible visions of my being part of it. Now all I could do was wonder if the old man's mad story about the SS was true. Had Becker not only eluded me but also achieved his true objective? I could easily imagine those cold eyes, that granite face not changing in the slightest as he killed the old man. Once again I'd let myself be distracted and overlooked the obvious. But what was the connection with the baroness and her lovers? That they were all Germans?

"Señor Marco, who sold me the beer, said a farmer went by the old man's place this morning and found him lying dead in his bed."

"Any sign that he was murdered?"

"Marco didn't say so. He did say López went there and came back and told the priest to go."

I looked up at the sun. Still hours to go before nightfall and only two full days left. "I'm going out to look," I said as I headed for my shack to change into long trousers.

"May I come with you?"

"Yes."

It was fortunate that Rojas had chosen to join me, because the priest was still there when we arrived. It was a peaceful scene except for the flies circling and attacking from all directions. The Crazy German was lying on his bed as if asleep, a slight smile on his face. There was no evidence of violence, nothing was broken that hadn't been for some time. A pot of stew hung over the now-dead embers out back, and the orphaned chickens and goats were calmly pursuing their perpetual, largely fruitless foraging. Rojas greeted the priest, who was standing scratching his head, and explained who I was.

"Do you think he was Catholic?" asked the priest sadly. "I never saw him at Mass. Most Germans are Protestants."

"He might have been," I replied. "Many Germans are Catholic."

"Yes. I sometimes forget that."

"Either way, did he ever harm anybody?"

"Not that I know of. He kept very much to himself."

"Then he wasn't a bad man."

"No. I'll ask God to judge him kindly and give him the benefit of the doubt. Not a Mass, of course, but a few words on his behalf."

"That would be good. Here," I said, handing him some sucres, "I hope this will cover the expenses."

The priest looked at the money. "It will more than cover it, thank you. I'll ask one of the neighbors to help prepare him, and we'll bury him tomorrow. Right here."

With his crisis solved, the priest set off to make arrangements while I knelt and examined the body. As far as I could tell there were no new wounds and no old ones that looked fatal. And no suspicious bruises. He could have been poisoned, I supposed, but would he have that slight smile on his face? I didn't know, but I doubted it. The man was old, and old men sometimes just die.

I looked around the room, but there wasn't much to see. The table, the chairs, and the rag-like clothes hanging from the wall. There was also a tin box, the kind candy comes in, on the floor in the corner. I put it on the table and opened it. Again, not much. Four small, ragged photographs of several middle-aged men and women and one child, who looked like a boy. The photos were well coated with greasy fingerprints. Aside from the photos there were several round, white pebbles, a Dutch passport, and what looked like a .30-caliber rifle casing.

I opened the passport. There was the Crazy German's photograph. He looked a few, but not many, years younger. I read on: Willem Beeckman, born in Amsterdam in 1872, occupation, businessman. There was only one immigration stamp indicating that Beeckman had entered Ecuador during the summer of 1929.

All very interesting, especially since I was certain the Crazy German wasn't Dutch. He spoke German like a German would. Or so it seemed to me. I picked up the rifle shell. Why would a German have a Dutch passport, and why would he save a shell casing from what was probably a hunting rifle? Could his story about the guy who killed the SS officer be true? Could he have been that guy? And if the story was true, had he really been crazy? Had he been driven over the edge by fear, loneliness, or even monumental self-satisfaction at a job well done? Or had he faked it all? I felt certain that I'd never know for sure; the truth about the man was just one more secret that Las Encantadas would keep. I decided on reflection, however, that he was probably no crazier than half the residents of the islands.

Whatever the truth of the Crazy German's story, it now seemed obvious that no matter who else he may or may not have killed, Becker had nothing to do with this old man's death.

I was even hotter, more tired, and more bug bitten when we got back to Wreck Bay than I had been before we went out to the Crazy German's. Once again, the bay's cool waters worked wonders, and by nine Seaman Rojas and I had decided to treat ourselves to another meal at the Miramar. The way things were going, I would only have the chance twice more. If I was lucky.

No matter what López's intentions were with regard to my future, as far as the public was concerned I remained the sergeant's friend and favorite, which meant we received our usual high level of service. And an increasing number of quick, suspicious glances from those around me.

The night was hot and muggy, and after returning to my rented hovel I spent it tossing and turning. I tried to think about Ana, but harsher, less attractive facets of reality kept intruding. The Guayaquil boat was due in two days, and I didn't want to be on it when it left. It was always possible that Don Vicente might be able to help, but that seemed a long shot. It certainly didn't worry López. Ana's father was rich and well established, but from what everybody said López might have stronger political backing.

I could squander my few remaining days of freedom going back and questioning everybody I'd already questioned, but I was certain that would lead nowhere. I had to find Becker and Sofía and talk to them. With luck, Ana might track down the maid, but I had to do something dramatic to corner the elusive German. At the same time I had to face the bitterest of the many bitter truths: even if I did provide López with the killer and a carload of convincing evidence, he was perfectly capable of still sending me to prison if it suited his mysterious purposes. Or he could send me back to New York. Or telegram New York and invite my many friends there to come visit.

Almost from the start I'd suspected that both López, and possibly the commandant, knew more than they were admitting to me or anybody else. López clearly had no intention of telling me anything about Becker. I had no choice but to see if the commandant would talk. He was the one who insisted he had to know more about the man, but I now felt certain he already knew more than he was saying.

I arrived at naval headquarters a little after nine in the morning, without having bothered with breakfast. The commandant's sedan was already there. I said good morning to Rojas, who was chatting with another sailor, and went directly in to the commandant's office. It must have been a slow day—I suspect the officer had many slow days out there in the middle of nowhere—because I was able to see him immediately. "Thank you for seeing me, sir."

"It is my pleasure. What do you have to tell me about this German?"

"Not as much as I'd like. I still haven't been able to catch up with him, although it appears that he is a geologist and is looking for some sort of minerals. We found some of his samples, and Miss de Guzmán thinks they might be a kind of tungsten ore."

"Tungsten? Yes, of course. She is a very clever young woman. It's a very important mineral for hardening steel. Becker's papers say he has permission to search for any minerals that interest him or his employer, the Krupp Group."

"What!" I gasped. "If you know what he's here for, why have you told me to find out what he's doing?"

"I know what he is supposed to be doing, Mr. Freiman, not what he is, in fact, doing."

"What do you think he might be up to? Trying to track down the man who killed a German officer years ago and came here to hide?"

"I understand that you talked to the Crazy German. He just died, did he not? Did you believe his story?"

"Yes. He was definitely German, yet he had a Dutch passport with a Dutch name that says he was born in Amsterdam. He also had a .30-caliber rifle shell that he seemed to be keeping as a memento."

"That proves nothing, but I am inclined to agree with you."

"So the mystery of Becker is solved."

"No, I fear not. There are other things, dangerous things, he might also be doing."

"What?"

"Gathering information about possible locations for German military or naval facilities. A submarine base, maybe. One that could be used against American shipping in the Pacific."

I felt like laughing. "You mean like Thompson, the American? He says he's looking for a site for a fish cannery, but his surveying instruments are the property of the United States War Department."

"Yes, the North American government is very worried about the Japanese, not just the Germans."

"This is insane!"

"I have thought so at times. My superiors favor a policy of working with your country, so naturally I do nothing to hinder Thompson. There are other factions who favor Germany and do what they can to assist people like Becker."

"Would any of those factions include López's superiors?"

"They might."

"Then you're no longer interested in Becker?"

"I still want you to find him. The way he keeps wandering around makes me and my superiors nervous."

"I think he killed the baroness and probably her two friends."

"Then you have two good reasons to find him."

And only two days to do it, I thought. And then a name hit me with all the force of Babe Ruth's bat. A name that had always been there, yet I'd totally overlooked it.

Pepe Hernández.

22

"Seaman Rojas," I demanded as I found my aide still chatting in front of the naval headquarters, "do you know a fisherman named Pepe Hernández?"

"No, sir. May I ask why?"

"Because Piers Hanson said Hernández has been ferrying Becker from island to island. When he was visiting the baroness, Hernández would have been there, or close by. He would have seen if Becker had any blood on him. Can you find out where he lives?"

"I'll try, sir." About half an hour later he returned to where I was waiting on the dock, watching some gulls fight over a long-dead fish head. "They say he lives right here, on San Cristóbal, a couple miles up the coast, but nobody's seen him in some time."

"Does he have a family?"

"A wife and two or three children."

"OK, we're going visiting. Do you think you can find the place?"

"There's a path that runs along the shore. We can just keep following it and asking until we find the right place."

I looked down at my feet and imagined the path we'd be following. "Is there a shoe store in Wreck Bay?"

"Señor Marco, the man who I've been buying our beer from, also has some shoes."

In addition to beer and shoes, Marco's tiny store sold local cigarettes, fishing hooks, canned peaches, bags of wheat, and just about every little odd or end I could think of. He didn't have many of each, but he had a few, so I ended up with a sturdy pair of locally made lace-up shoes. I also bought several pairs of socks, since the shoes were far too big.

As advertised, the path led along the rocky, sandy, treeless shore. Not knowing what we were looking for, Rojas asked questions at every little shack we came to, and we did, eventually, find Pepe Hernández's small house. It was the sixth one we came to and, to give Pepe credit, it was the best maintained. The siding was weathered and had clearly never seen an ounce of paint, but there was a small garden, and several small trees had been planted and nurtured. Our arrival was announced by the frantic barking of a small tan dog and carefully monitored by two almost naked children with huge eyes. They looked to be about four or five at most. One was a boy and one a girl. A worn middle-aged woman stepped out of the little wooden house and waited. Rojas walked up to her and introduced us. I noticed that when the seaman said "López" the woman frowned.

"My husband isn't here," she told him.

"Is he off fishing?"

"No, a gringo, a foreigner, hired him to take him around the different islands."

"How did the foreigner find him?"

The woman glanced back and forth between us. "Sergeant López. We needed the money." She sounded embarrassed, almost apologetic.

"Have you seen your husband since he started working for the foreigner?"

"They have been back several times. I see him briefly."

"What does he say about the foreigner and what they're doing?"

"He says the man is harsh and impatient. He doesn't completely understand what he is doing. Collecting rocks. Looking around. Drawing maps."

"Do you know where he is now?"

"Has he done something wrong?"

Rojas glanced back at me. I nodded, and he continued, "Very definitely not. We're trying to find the gringo to deliver an important message."

The woman looked at Rojas skeptically, as would anybody who knew or suspected we were working for Sergeant López, but the seaman's marvelously innocent expression seemed to win out. "He sent word that they would be back in another day or two. He's been gone so long. I want him back. And so do the children."

Rojas looked around at the house and the healthy-looking vegetable garden that enlivened the otherwise bleak yard. "I'm sure he'll be happy to be home after so long and will be proud of how you've kept the house and garden in his absence."

"I hope so."

And I hoped so too, since I now suspected it was the wife who not only worked the garden, tended the children, and kept the place tidy but who had also made the effort to create a little beauty with the trees.

"Are you sure he'll be back in a day or two?"

"Yes. He said the gringo has to catch the next boat to Guayaquil."

I'd better not be with him, I thought glumly.

"Is there any message you want me to give him?"

Again, Rojas looked at me. "Tell her there's no special message, although she might mention to the gringo that Sergeant López was getting a little worried about him."

The seaman paused a moment, furrowing his brow slightly as he glanced at me, then repeated the lie.

When we got back to Wreck Bay, Rojas and I naturally decided to celebrate regaining Becker's trail by a good dinner at our favorite restaurant, but first I stopped at home to take advantage of the "sea cure" I was finding so essential for my mental health. On my way back from the beach I encountered my landlord, the tailor. I smiled at him and said *buenas noches*, one of my growing collection of Spanish phrases.

"*Buenas noches, señor Freiman*," he responded, eyeing my new clothes. "New clothes. Who do alterations?" he asked in very broken English.

"A friend, Señor Ramos, but when I need more I'll be sure to bring them to you."

"Yes, *por favor*." From his expression I think he was worried that new competition may have suddenly appeared in the settlement.

We nodded again and each proceeded on his way.

Eating at the Miramar had come to seem like eating at home. The food was good, the setting rustic but attractive, and the spirit lively. That's why I'd let it grow on me. Even though we arrived early, long before the combo had even finished their own dinner, and left long before the action really heated up, the night proved to be both memorable and instructive.

When I arrived, Rojas was already seated at "our" table. "You see, Seaman, it's true. The more time you spend with me, the more important a person you become. Now you have your own table at the Miramar. May I join you?"

"My pleasure, sir."

The night was hot, and the air was dead except for massive squadrons of flies and gnats.

"Rojas," I asked in a very low voice, slapping a housefly to death on the table, "has it occurred to you that Sergeant López may have killed the baroness?"

My aide looked hurriedly around. "It has, sir, but why would he?"

"He's a man, to begin with, and it seems just about every man in the islands was involved with the woman. And I'm certain he can be violent."

"Nobody has mentioned seeing him there the day she was killed."

"Perhaps Sofía saw him. That may be why she's made it so difficult for anybody to find her." As I said it I felt a twinge in my chest. Why hadn't I heard anything from Ana? What the hell was she up to? Had she managed, despite her cleverness, to get herself in trouble?

"Then we must hope the doña manages to find her."

"Yes. But there's another possibility to consider. From what the commandant tells me and from what we've learned, Becker is a geologist working for a big German corporation. He has permission to look for minerals. Indeed, one faction in the capital, the pro-German one, seems to be backing him. I also understand that López is supported by that same faction. From the way he keeps telling me Becker didn't kill her I suspect he's Becker's guardian angel. Is it possible that Becker killed the baroness and then López killed Ritter and Ernst to make sure they hadn't seen anything? We know Becker was there."

"Why would Becker kill her?"

"Like López, he's a man with a temper. And she, or so everybody says, also had a temper and sometimes insisted on being the boss."

"Sir, now you're worrying me. I can see what you want to do next."

"I'm afraid so. We have to investigate López, learn more about him. Find out where he was the night the baroness was killed and also the night Ritter and Ernst were killed."

"This is going to be very dangerous, sir. Even for a nobody like me."

The hot, damp night was shattered by a trumpet blast. The combo had just finished its dinner, and the trumpeter was clearing his lungs and preparing us all for a night of island revelry.

"You want to jump ship? Not go any further with me?"

"Yes, sir, that's what I want to do, but I won't. I'll continue on with you, but remember that I would like to live so someday I can have a wife and a family and a career."

"That makes two of us, Seaman."

I looked at his face and for the first time saw real fear on it. I felt sick. I was dragging Ana and Rojas into the mud, a burning, acidic mud, with me, and it all had started when I shot that punk in Hell's Kitchen and then stole Alf's boat.

"Do you see Esme over there, sir, at that table with two other girls?"

I looked and nodded.

"López became very angry last night; nobody's sure why, but they say he almost beat her to death. He's never done that before to one of his girls. The only reason she's alive is that she makes money for him."

I peered across the space at the girl and thought I could see discolorations on her face. She also seemed to be holding her arm strangely. "Do you think she'll talk to us?"

"She'd have to be insane."

"Go over and ask her."

Rojas took a deep breath, stood, and walked over toward the girls just as the combo stopped tuning and launched into a raucous tango. I watched as he approached the table and, nodding slightly, started talking to Esme. At first she didn't appear to pay the slightest attention, but suddenly she exploded, shouting and waving her fists in the air. A moment later Rojas was ushering the still-fulminating girl in my direction. I stood as she approached the table and offered her Rojas's chair, but the Miramar management was ahead of us—a third chair magically appeared before the girl reached it.

"*Buenas noches,*" I said. Esme laughed bitterly, then took the chair. Close up, the damage was appalling—her face was both bruised and lacerated, it looked like a tooth or two was missing, and something was wrong with her arm and also with one leg.

"Thank you for talking to me," I said, then waited for Rojas to translate.

"Why not? I'd kill the son of a bitch if I could. Rojas says that even though you work for López you're not his friend."

"You believe him?"

"Rojas is a good boy. I believe him."

"Still, being seen talking to me might be very dangerous for you."

"If he kills me, he kills me," she snarled. "I've got nothing to lose. If I'm lucky I'll live to take the Guayaquil boat to the mainland. I have money for the fare."

And then what, I wondered. Working the streets of Guaya-quil, which I knew was a big, rough seaport, would be like working the streets of the worst parts of Manhattan. It would be a very big change from Wreck Bay, which might be poor but was far from violent. Except maybe for López.

"Do you know where López was the night the German baroness was murdered on Floreana?"

"He was with me at about sunset in the plaza, collecting part of what I'd already earned."

"And after that?"

"I don't know. I didn't see him until the next morning when he collected again."

"And that night?

"The same. It's always the same. It may have been earlier than usual, I can't remember."

While she answered I looked around to see if anybody interesting was watching us, but I didn't see anybody I rec-ognized. I then realized that Esme hadn't even bothered to look around. She really didn't seem to care about the risk.

"So you have no idea what he did after collecting from you?"

"No."

"Do you think he was seeing the baroness?"

"For sex?"

"Yes."

"Impossible! She liked to make her men crawl, and López is one man who does not crawl."

"Do you know a German named Becker?"

She paused a moment, then replied, "Yes, he spent the night with me about a month ago."

"Does he like being humiliated?"

"Not by me, but he's very strange."

"Strange?"

"Very precise. Everything has to be exactly the way he wants it. First this, then that."

I wasn't quite sure what to ask next. Esme had told me a great deal, but I was going to have to think about it before I was sure what she'd really told me. I believed that by losing control and beating up Esme, López had made his first serious error; he'd revealed that he was feeling pressure. Maybe it was his second error, I added to myself. Leaving the rocks and the DKW manual out where I could see them might have been his first, although it was possible he'd done it on purpose for some reason. No, I was being far too clever!

The pressure López felt might, of course, have been related to the governor's suicide, but I doubted it. I hoped that it was the result of my closing in on Becker. And on López himself. I hoped the pressure would get to him and he would make more, and bigger, mistakes. And make them quickly. I didn't want to be on the next boat to Guayaquil with Esme. "Thank you."

"Did I help you? Are you going to get the fucker? Maybe he did kill the German woman."

"Maybe."

And then she was on her feet. Without saying another word, she turned and walked back to her friends at the table.

Our food arrived, and I played with mine a few minutes while the lanterns suspended along the open side of the restaurant began to dance in the salty breeze.

"What do we do now, sir?"

"I'm not sure, Rojas. We can't just march up to López and accuse him of murder. We're going to learn more about him, like what he's doing when he disappears. And we're going to talk to Becker somehow. We're also going to do something to keep that girl alive at least until she can get on the boat."

"I can tell you what he does part of the time we don't see him—he goes from island to island and settlement to settlement looking them over and making sure there are no problems. He also has many business deals with people, and he watches over them."

"What sort of business deals?"

"Those girls, for one. He's also part owner of some fishing boats and owns some houses and buildings. And he loans money to people. Even sailors."

"And he always gets paid back, right?"

"Always, sir."

"Have you ever borrowed money from him?"

Rojas squirmed.

"Is that why you spy for him?"

"I spy for him mainly because he's a very powerful man here. I have no choice."

Cops, I thought. We come in all shapes and sizes. López and Sergeant McGrath were like two peas in a pod. If they knew each other, they'd either be good pals or mortal rivals.

I watched the lanterns dance and felt a sinking sensation. The obvious way to find out more about López—where he was and when—was to track down his various business contacts. From what Rojas said, it sounded as if there were dozens spread out all over the archipelago, and I had no time to work my way through even a small portion of them. I looked at Rojas a moment and sighed. The logical place to start was the busy sergeant's contacts at Wreck Bay and on Floreana, such as the owners of a couple restaurants who seemed to go out of their way to please him. They probably owed him money, or he might even be a partner.

There's no time like the present, I thought. "The man who owns this place, García, seems very interested in keeping on López's good side."

"Yes, sir." Rojas now looked more uncomfortable than ever. "Nobody in the islands wants any trouble with him."

Except possibly a Norwegian and a couple working girls. The Miramar looked quite prosperous to me, but I knew that thugs preferred to participate in prosperous businesses. Somehow, they always managed to find a way of elbowing in even if the owner didn't need a loan. "Ask her if Señor García would join us for a few minutes," I directed Rojas as I waved for the waitress.

"You *are* going to get us killed, sir. Just as soon as López hears that you're asking questions about him."

"Time's running out, and he's beginning to make mistakes. Anyway, I'm sure you'll survive."

He stared at me a moment, then repeated the request to the waitress.

"Is there a problem, sir?" asked García as he scurried up to the table. He looked a little harried, as well he might be managing a place like the Miramar.

"None at all. The seaman and I both love your restaurant."

"Thank you, sir." He turned and started to leave.

"Please join us, señor," I insisted.

"Thank you but I must attend to the other customers."

"Please," I said, glowering at him.

He thought about it for a moment, then sat down. I looked at him, trying to decide how to start. I was suddenly more aware of the passing of time than I ever had been. Every second was etched in my awareness. "Your time is valuable, Señor García, and so is mine, so I'll come right to the point:

Is Sergeant López a business associate of yours? Is he a partner in the Miramar?"

García drew back as if I'd slapped him. "That is none of your affair."

"Do you know where he was the night the baroness was killed?"

"He was here." He stood and walked away.

I didn't believe him.

Rojas looked at me with the haunted expression of a condemned man. Reconciled, perhaps, but still condemned. "The sergeant will know you have been asking about him within an hour."

"Yes. We're committed now. We have to move quickly. Do you think Pepe Hernández may have borrowed money from López?"

"It's possible, sir, but I have no way of knowing for sure. His wife did say they needed money, but so does everybody."

"Still, it makes sense. López told Hernández to ferry Becker around, and Hernández figured he had no choice."

"That seems logical, sir."

"Tomorrow we'll talk to Pepe's wife again. And what about the people on Floreana? Like Elías?"

Rojas mumbled something.

"Please speak up."

"If we're still alive tomorrow."

"I think we will be."

"So we have two people to talk to."

"Is it possible that he might have business dealings with the Herzogs or any of the other European settlers?"

"I don't know, sir, although that seems less likely."

I was about to lay out a plan of action for the next day when I spotted a commotion at the bar. I looked more closely and realized that Gregor Herzog was the center of the action. He was dressed in shorts and a long-sleeved shirt and—how else can I describe it?—was cavorting with one arm around a very pretty Ecuadorean girl. The girl was much better dressed than Esme and her friends. Gregor was waving his other arm and seemed to be almost dancing. He was very drunk, although no more than I had been the other night. I was still chuckling when he caught sight of me. "Fred," he shouted across the night as he let go of the girl and staggered over to our table.

"How's the fishing, Gregor?" I asked, glancing at the girl.

"I've been fishing my brains out all week." He slurred slightly as he spoke and didn't seem to catch my joke. "And I've got damn little to show for it. But there'll be better days. I'm taking a holiday tonight before I go back home." He winked. "How's your fishing going?"

"I still haven't caught the big one yet."

"You will." As he paused, the stupid smile on his face disappeared. "Fred, I must talk with you in private, but not now. I must tell you something that I don't want others, especially Carla, to hear. I'll see you later."

Before I could pin him down, he danced off back to the girl. Within a few minutes they'd disappeared. We waited another hour. "OK," I finally said, "we don't have time to wait anymore for Gregor. He'll just have to find me when he's ready. We have to talk to the commandant now, before López learns we're sorting through his affairs."

"Tonight? He'll be home in bed most likely."

"Tonight. Do you know where he lives?"

"Along the shore. Several miles from Wreck Bay. It's a long walk."

"Near the governor's mansion?" I hoped not. I didn't want to be anywhere near López at the moment.

23

As Rojas predicted, it was a long walk. The night was moonless and filled with a true sea fog that went well beyond the normal mist. It was the sort of night when it's easy to trip over the stones, large and small, that grow like weeds in what passes for roads in Las Encantadas. Fortunately, my new shoes were up to the job, although I did end up with a bumper crop of blisters.

It was well after midnight when my guide spotted the small, hazy light in the more intense blob of darkness that marked the commandant's house. I started to relax at the sight of our destination, to let down my guard, and my pulse began to return to normal. Then my heart stuttered when I recognized the muted, irregular snarl of a motorcycle approaching us from behind, picking its way among the various dangers of the road. I turned and saw the bike's headlight, still faint, bobbing and twisting in the surrounding darkness. "Off the road and crouch down like you're a rock," I hissed to Rojas. He'd already taken at least one step in the right direction before I finished speaking.

We crouched, holding our breaths and trying to turn ourselves into faceless stones, as the shadowy form of a big motorcycle and rider crept up on us. Shit, I thought, clenching my fists, it had to be López, and he was going to the commandant's. Had García already told him I was prying? Were Rojas and I walking into a trap? Were López and the commandant working together? If so, then I'd soon be dead. And probably Rojas, too. And Ana and Don Vicente would be fighting for their lives.

The growling shadow came alongside and then passed on down the road, the driver clearly more interested in the stones on the road than those sitting alongside it. I gulped a lungful of air and held it again as the shadow reached the light of the commandant's quarters. Would it pull off the road? No, it continued on, and I exhaled far too loudly. I turned and could see Rojas's eyes fixed on me. "Let's get moving before I have a heart attack."

I sensed more than saw motion near the light. A voice called out what sounded like a challenge. Rojas identified us and told the sentry that we had very important business with the commandant. "I know that sailor," explained Rojas in a low voice. "I think we woke him up."

After pondering a moment, the sentry told us to wait. He pounded on the door. A household servant opened it and told us to wait in the vestibule while he went for the commandant. The officer soon appeared, wearing a blue bathrobe. Much to my relief he seemed in no way put out by being dragged out of bed at two in the morning. "I understand you have something of great urgency to report, Mr. Freiman."

"I do, sir, and I'm afraid you're not going to like it."

The commandant smiled briefly. Almost chuckled. "Then please come into my office. You also, Seaman. May I offer you coffee or wine or perhaps a glass of rum?"

I requested rum. Rojas, who knew the value of behaving himself when faced with authority, asked for coffee. The commandant rang a small bell, and the servant who'd opened the door reappeared. Our host told him what was required, and it was delivered almost immediately. The commandant then settled back to listen.

"Sir," I said, "I still haven't been able to talk to Becker, although I understand he's due back any time now so he can catch the next Guayaquil boat.

"However," I continued quickly, "it's becoming very clear that Sergeant López is in charge of watching over him."

"Yes, I have assumed that for some time."

"Did you know López speaks German?"

"No. Does he?"

"Yes. I now also think López is involved in the murders of the baroness and her two friends. He may be the murderer himself."

"Oh," said the commandant, sitting forward. This seemed to be what he'd been hoping to hear.

I spent the next fifteen minutes laying out all we'd learned and the conclusions we'd reached. Once or twice the commandant asked Rojas to clarify a point or two in Spanish, but otherwise he followed my account intently.

"Interesting! That is all very interesting, but it is not solid proof."

"No, sir, it's not. But if I do manage to get solid proof, would you arrest Sergeant López for one or more murders?"

The commandant looked at the ceiling. "On paper I have almost absolute power out here. In reality, thanks to the games the politicians play in Quito, my power is not as absolute as it might be. If you can convince me that López has murdered somebody, even those worthless Germans, I will arrest him and send him to the mainland for trial. There will be complications, but reality must be confronted."

"Thank you, sir. And one other thing. The girl Esme . . ."

"The prostitute?"

"Yes. She works for López, and he beat the living daylights out of her last night."

"It sounds as if the sergeant is losing his self-control."

"She also spoke with Rojas and me publicly at the Miramar earlier this evening. She intends to leave, to go to Guayaquil."

"I am sorry to hear that. She has never been a problem that I know of. Life will be very, very hard for her there."

"Her information was valuable to me, but now I'm worried about her safety. Is there any way you can protect her until she gets on the boat?"

"Has she asked for protection?"

"She's still very angry. She's asked for nothing."

The commandant, who was proving far more clever than I'd ever dreamed he would be, thought for a moment. "I will arrest her for practicing her trade in my headquarters and hold her in my cells."

Rojas struggled to stifle a laugh. I think he might have been nervous sitting in the commandant's house.

"Has she ever done that?" I asked.

"Not that I know of, but nobody will argue with me. At least not for a few days."

"Sir, I want to thank you," I said, rising.

"My pleasure. You do realize that many eyes will be on the Guayaquil boat when she sails. Will you and Esme be going ashore along with Herr Becker, or will Sergeant López be going with the man he has been protecting for so many weeks?"

The commandant clearly saw some humor in the possibilities. I, for some reason, did not.

I was up early the next morning, certain that López and Becker would appear at some point during the day. Where, precisely, they would first show up was uncertain, so I sent Rojas to watch the governor's house after recruiting his buddy Gonzales, who was off duty, to watch Pepe Hernández's house. I would keep an eye on the dock and plaza in the settlement. If either of the two sailors spotted one or the other of our quarry he would come report to me. I hoped to find a way of talking to Becker without López getting in the way.

Not expecting anything much to happen until later in the day, I changed into my swim shorts and headed for the beach. I was walking past my landlord's little shop when I ran right into the man I'd been hunting for a week. He was striding toward me, as if he were on a parade ground, a business suit over his left arm. "Herr Becker," I greeted him in German.

He stopped and looked me up and down with the same expression of distaste he'd shown the last time. "So, Herr Freiman, you have finally caught up with me, despite Sergeant López's bumbling. He will be upset."

"You're up and out early," I observed, thinking that he and Hernández must have arrived around the time Rojas and I left the commandant's home office.

"I've lost weight and want this suit altered. I won't be seen wearing a baggy suit. López thinks you believe I killed the Baroness von Arndt. In fact, I get the feeling the monkey himself believes I did it."

And that was the key, although it took me a minute to spot it. One of my guesses had been right.

"Did you?"

"Of course not."

"Did you see her the day she was killed?"

"I've seen her many times; she was beautiful and amusing, despite her temper."

"Did you see her that day?"

I thought at first that he was going to refuse to answer, but he surprised me. "Yes, in the evening. After a while, I tired of her games. I had no desire to continue playing the role of the love slave. I told her so, and she became more demanding. She forgot her place. I became angry and left. She was still alive."

"How can I believe you?"

"You are German, I am German. Of course you believe me." He glowered at me a moment. "Ask the fisherman, Hernández, although why you might believe an Ecuadorean fisherman but not me I can't understand."

"I believe all sorts of people."

"Look here, Freiman. My work in this place is finished. The boat to the mainland arrives tomorrow, and when it leaves I'll be on it, and I can't tell you how pleased I'll be. Important things are happening in Germany. The geology here is fascinating, but the people are aboriginal, and having that fool López ordering me around and interfering with my work while claiming to be protecting me has been intolerable."

With that he turned and marched rapidly toward the tailor's shop. I didn't want to, but I believed him. It's hard to fake arrogance like that, and in my experience truly arrogant men don't usually bother to lie. They throw the awful truth in your face and dare you to do something about it. I considered trying to contact Rojas and Gonzales but decided to leave them where they were. Who knew what they might stumble on.

I couldn't help but feel a certain satisfaction as I waded out into the chill waters of Wreck Bay for my delayed morning swim. I still didn't have enough to hang López—or whatever it is they really do to murderers in Ecuador—but I was now confident he was my man. The sergeant had killed the baroness and then her two friends.

It was an excellent, bracing swim, and I felt extra clean as I headed back to my shack.

Almost as soon as I walked in the door my satisfaction collapsed utterly, like an automobile tire that had suffered a blowout. Sitting on my one chair, with his elbows on the rickety table and his head between his hands, was Gregor Herzog. "Gregor," I said cheerfully, "it's good to see you."

He looked up at me, his bloodshot eyes filled with pain, and I knew I'd spoken too loudly.

"Fred, the Guayaquil boat arrives tomorrow, and I don't want to see you leaving on it under arrest. There's something I must tell you, but you must make sure that Carla never learns what I'm about to say. She'll kill me. Or worse, leave me. You must promise."

I sat down on the bed, knowing I wasn't going to like where this was going. How could I promise when I didn't know what he was going to tell me? I went ahead and promised.

"I have some fish traps set off the shore of Floreana, not far from the baroness's house. I was working them the afternoon of the day she was killed. Some needed repairs, so I was there longer than I'd expected. I decided to stay, to sleep aboard the boat or maybe on the beach—that's something we do all the time around here. And then I got a little lonely and . . . you know . . . so I decided to visit her. I've done it before. Sometimes I find her games amusing, sometimes not. And she's so very lonely too. I often feel sorry for her."

"What!" I practically shouted. Once again reality seemed to be exploding in my face.

Gregor stared at me a moment. "Her life's been shit," he continued. "Her father was a successful merchant who was ruined by the war and committed suicide. Her mother then died of influenza, and she was forced to live, to survive, as best she could in that cesspool that was Germany. Remember, I was there too, so I know what I'm talking about. It was the winters that were hardest. She even had to walk the streets for a while to eat. Then she married an ancient baron, von Arndt, who was a Nazi, but the wrong kind of Nazi. He was killed in the Night of the Long Knives, in 1934, when Hitler decided to get rid of the undesirables in his party. She grabbed what she could and ran. Came here to get away, to live."

Ana had been right, I thought. About the photos and about the baroness.

"Where did Ritter and Ernst come from?"

"She never told me."

"Why did she tell you all this and nobody else?"

"Because nobody else was willing to listen. They took her at face value, and she could be very unpleasant."

I groaned inwardly at my ignorance.

"Anyway, when I got near the house I could see through the window that she already had a guest: Elías."

"Elías the cook?"

"Yes, and they were playing one of her games, or so I thought. She seemed to be shouting at him and whipping him with her riding crop. I decided that was not my game, and since she already had a playmate I returned to my boat and went to sleep. Early the next morning I checked my traps again and returned home."

"So you think Elías killed her?"

"It seems likely."

Thompson, Becker, Elías. How many other visitors could she possibly have in one day?

"Why didn't you tell me this before?"

"Isn't that obvious? I only tell you now so you can maybe save yourself."

So much for certainties. "Thanks, Gregor. I have to get to Floreana and talk to Elías fast. You don't look very good—probably shouldn't try to sail home today. Feel free to use my bed."

"Thanks," groaned Gregor. Spitting out the truth didn't seem to reduce his suffering one bit.

I changed into pants, shoes, and a shirt and was out the door before Gregor had managed to drag himself to my bed. When I arrived at naval headquarters the commandant was out, but the petty officer on duty seemed willing to try to help. Talking slowly and using my fifty-word Spanish vocabulary, I managed to get him to send a sailor to find Rojas and get him back to Wreck Bay and another to alert the gunboat skipper that we'd be heading for Floreana immediately. As I struggled to be understood I couldn't drive away the thought that somewhere, not so far over the horizon to the east, the Guayaquil boat was already on its way toward us.

We arrived off Blackwater Bay early in the afternoon after a quick passage over the rolling, deep blue sea. I examined the small settlement through the skipper's binoculars and saw few signs of life. I made another pass and spotted Piers Hanson sitting on his porch with a rifle in his lap. "Rojas, do you know how to handle a pistol?"

"Yes, sir."

"Good. Ask the skipper to issue you one and tell him that he's going ashore with us. Armed. And the oarsmen are to bring rifles, too."

"It looks so calm there, sir."

"It does, but it isn't. See Piers Hanson sitting on his porch with that rifle in his lap?"

"I'm sure we can deal with it, sir." The kid was a firm, devoted comrade again, and undoubtedly would be right up to the second we both got killed.

"I hope so."

The skipper shrugged and did as I asked. For a moment I thought I saw a faint smile appear on his face. I guess he was getting used to me. Or maybe there was somebody at Blackwater Bay he didn't like.

As we rowed in, I kept my eyes on Hanson—the son of a bitch had said he was going to get even—but he didn't move. The boat slid onto the beach, and the oarsmen jumped out and dragged the bow up into the sand. They then grabbed their rifles while they held the boat to let us climb out. The beach was empty except for two small fishing boats that were obviously in need of repair.

I walked slowly inland, Rojas and the skipper following close behind. All with drawn weapons. Hanson remained motionless. We turned and headed for Elías's house. I knocked on the door, then shoved it open to find the cook lying in his bed, staring blankly at the ceiling through bloodshot eyes. The room stank of rum and urine.

"Elías," I snapped, with Rojas translating, "do you hear me?"

He turned his head slightly but said nothing.

"You were seen the night the baroness was killed. You were with her, playing one of her games."

"That fucking German's been hounding me night and day," he replied without taking his eyes off the ceiling. "With his gun. I can't go out. I can't take a piss. Every time I show myself, he aims and sometimes he fires." I could see that he was shaking.

"Did you kill the baroness?"

"We're all better off without her. Ask anybody on this island," he mumbled. "If you arrest me, will you keep Hanson away from me?"

"Did you kill her?"

"Yes. She said I'd stolen some money from her and started whipping me. Just like the other Germans. I didn't steal anything. She was taking away my manhood, the bitch. I killed her." He said it all while continuing to stare at the ceiling, and I couldn't help but wonder whether he'd really stolen the money or not.

"Did you kill Ritter and Ernst?"

He stared at me a moment, as if I were a fool. "No. Of course not. They were up at the shack where she sends them when she has guests."

I had no choice but to believe him, I decided. Ritter and Ernst were killed the night after the baroness died. And the sailor tending *Pegasus* said he'd heard arguing in what sounded like either German or English. Elías spoke neither, so I was back to López, who spoke both.

"Arrest him," I said, looking at the skipper and expecting Rojas to translate. I wasn't really sure if the petty officer had the authority or the experience to execute the arrest, but it turned out that he had both. He took Elías by the arm and said something to him. The cook sighed and nodded and tried to stand. With the help of Rojas and the skipper he managed to stagger out to the beach, where he was loaded into the boat and taken out to the gunboat. While I was waiting for my ride, I walked over to Hanson.

"So you got the little pig," he said. "Now I have to get you, which I will."

I should have shot him right then and there, while his gun was still lying in his lap. If somebody says he's hunting you, then you have to kill him before he succeeds. Just as a matter of policy. But I didn't. "Yes," I said. "The time will come." I turned and walked back down the beach, expecting to hear the crack of the rifle an instant before my back was blasted to shreds. Nothing happened, but I knew that if I was to stay in the islands something would have to be done about Piers Hanson.

I should have been happy as we headed back to Wreck Bay, but I wasn't. I had the baroness's killer cold, but that didn't even begin to solve my problem. I was convinced López had killed the two Germans, but I had no way of proving it. Under the circumstances, the sergeant had to protect himself; he had to send me ashore for trial for all three murders, no matter how much evidence there was of Elías's guilt. And, thanks to the magic of real-life politics, there would be nothing even the commandant could do unless I could show him the most solid possible evidence of López's guilt. I couldn't, and there was only one day left.

24

I watched the gunboat skipper lead Elías down the Wreck Bay dock and over to naval headquarters with a momentary sense of almost professional pride. I'd nabbed the fellow! However, I wasn't happy that it was Elías. He was a vicious hothead and I had no fondness for him, but I suspected he'd been pushed to the edge by both Piers Hanson and maybe by the baroness herself. I'd have much preferred to see Becker headed for the cell. Unfortunately, I was confident that the Nazi geologist was innocent. And setting pride aside, I was still headed for trial on the mainland for murder. If not for the baroness's, then for that of her friends.

"Let's get a beer," I said to Rojas. "We've worked hard today."

"Yes, sir. Do you have a plan how to get López before he gets you?" I like to think the only reason my assistant insisted on ruining my brief pleasure was that he was scared about his own skin and was trying to be constructive.

"No," I admitted. "Maybe a beer will help."

The combo was hard at work when we arrived at the Miramar, and to my great surprise, considering my last conversation with García, we received the usual attentive service. But even before we'd managed to sit, it was clear that something had changed. It was the other customers. Normally they'd frown briefly at us, then turn back to their business. Tonight, many were staring hard at us and clearly talking about us. Word of Elías's arrest must have preceded us, and I'd fallen yet one more notch in their estimation. Yesterday I was the lackey of the intensely disliked López. Today, I was the oppressor of one of their fellow citizens. Whatever Elías's reputation among the other islanders, he was Ecuadorean, one of them. I was another German interloper. "I think I made some enemies today," I said to my companion.

"Fortunately for me, sir, I'm not an important person. Nobody notices me."

"Don't believe it! Usually it's the small fish who end up getting caught and fried. The important people are too important to be inconvenienced."

We finished our beers and left. After saying good night to Rojas, I returned to my shack, expecting to find Gregor embalmed on my bed. Gregor wasn't there, but Ana was. Sitting at the table reading a book by the feeble light of the kerosene lamp. She looked tired and disheveled.

Overwhelmed by a sense of relief, and feeling a little foolish about it, I leaned over and kissed her on the neck. She turned and looked up, and I kissed her properly. She smiled and kissed me back. "I've been worried about you," I said.

"You shouldn't have been. I live here, remember."

"I'd heard nothing from you, and this whole affair has become very dirty," I explained, sitting down on the bed.

"They say you arrested Elías, the cook, for killing the baroness." She closed the book as she spoke.

"That's true."

"What about Becker?"

"He's here someplace, waiting for the Guayaquil boat. He didn't do it."

"How do you know?"

"Because Elías admitted it, and we have a witness: Gregor."

"Gregor?"

I repeated Gregor's account of the night the baroness was killed.

"Poor Gregor," she said with a sad expression. "When she finds out, Carla will make him suffer all the furies of hell."

"How's she going to find out?"

"She will, somehow. Gregor will probably blab it to her himself."

"Unfortunately," I observed, not terribly interested at the moment in Gregor's self-inflicted misfortune, "I still think López killed the love slaves, but I've got to prove it before he ships *me* off to hell. The key is Becker. He said López thinks that he killed the baroness, and López was supposed to be keeping him out of trouble. I think López killed Ritter and Ernst to cover for Becker, but I'm not sure how to prove it."

"This is your lucky day, then, because I've got a witness who says just that."

"You found Sofía?"

"She's hiding because she's terrified of López. She was cleaning up late in the evening after the baroness was killed when Ritter and Ernst came into the house and told her to finish up and leave. Just before heading home, she saw López come up from the beach and force his way into the house. There was a lot of shouting, in German she thinks, then gunfire. She ran all the way home and packed a few things, then went to one of her cousins and insisted that he take her to other cousins on Isabela."

"Will she talk to us?"

"For now only to me. Papa has done business with some of her relatives, and she remembers me when I was small. She trusts me."

There was nothing I could think of to say, so I hugged her and kissed her again.

Ana and I practically ran across the plaza to naval headquarters with Roberto, who'd been outside the shack all the time, one step behind. The commandant had left for the day. Ana asked the duty petty officer to call him at home. From the look on his face I'm sure he would have done anything she asked. Five minutes later we were packed into the cab of the navy's official stake truck, bouncing over the road out to the commandant's house. The ride, with Rojas's friend Gonzales at the wheel, was even rougher and more uncomfortable than the walk had been the night before.

When we arrived, the commandant was waiting in his office. He bowed slightly to Ana and nodded to me. "Doña Ana, Mr. Freiman, you say you have a witness to Sergeant López's murdering the baroness's two friends?"

I reported what Becker had said, then Ana described locating Sofía and what the maid had told her.

"Will she repeat all of this to me?" asked the naval officer. He was trying to keep a look of concern on his face, but he wasn't able to totally hide his satisfaction.

"Yes, sir, although she'll feel better if López is in jail."

"I will arrest him immediately; then she will tell me?"

"She might be more comfortable on Isabela."

"Why not! I will go to Isabela to speak with her. This is going to cause all sorts of political problems, so I must have all the information. But it must be done." The more he spoke the more obvious his relief, and even pleasure, became. The commandant and his superiors in Quito must have been hoping for something just like this to improve their board position in the political chess game.

When the commandant said immediately, it turned out, he meant *immediately*. After arming himself and Gonzales, he handed Ana a shotgun and rounded up his sentry, and we all piled into his car and the stake truck and headed for the governor's mansion.

It was dark when we stopped at the front steps. Without waiting, the commandant jumped out of the car and walked around to the side door. He threw that open and marched down the hall with the rest of us following. As we approached the office we could hear an argument raging in German. Again, the commandant threw open the door, and we found López and Becker standing on either side of the desk shouting face-to-face.

"Sergeant López," snapped the naval officer. López, whose pistol was at his hip, turned. Becker glanced sideways at the commandant, then drew his own weapon and fired point-blank at López's chest. Before any of us could raise our own guns, the German had laid his down on the desk and, without looking again at the commandant, turned to me. "This subhuman fool killed those two degenerates because he thought I'd killed the baroness and he needed to protect me. His stupidity has almost destroyed my mission."

We stood there a moment, stunned. Finally the commandant recovered and, after picking up the German's pistol, told Becker he was under arrest. Becker nodded, almost clicked his heels, and marched out of the room with the rest of us following.

The next day, about noon, Rojas and I watched as the Guayaquil boat pulled into Wreck Bay. I can't say he was totally reconciled to having missed the shootout, but he was a flexible kid and seemed to be recovering fast.

To say that the four deaths—the baroness, Ritter, Ernst, and López—caused a minor political problem would be an understatement. The government in Quito recognized the problem immediately. Rather than drag everybody from the commandant down ashore, where the whole confused mess would become public almost instantly, a special investigating magistrate was sent in a high-speed destroyer to limit the damage.

The magistrate, a very distinguished gentleman named Don Francisco Montaña, was known, by reputation if not in person, to Don Vicente and the commandant. Both agreed that, thanks to his exquisite sense of political balance, he was the best possible man for the job. Don Francisco was also a very fast and skillful worker. In the course of four or five days, he interviewed all of us. Even Sofía had agreed to come and speak to him at naval headquarters once Ana convinced her that López was truly dead. He also visited the castle and spoke with a number of the residents of Blackwater Bay.

Partway through the inquiry, López was buried at a surprisingly well-attended funeral. From what I was told, dozens of his debtors and unwilling partners—including Esme and her friends—showed up. Just to make sure he was really gone forever.

In the end, Don Francisco ruled that Elías had been provoked. The cook was convicted of manslaughter and sent to prison for one year. Don Francisco went on to ask Herr Becker to please take his ore samples and leave the islands immediately, on the boat to the mainland, which the magistrate had held at Wreck Bay until he completed his deliberations. He concluded by sentencing Piers Hanson to six months for assault. He then attended a good-bye party at the commandant's quarters and the next day boarded the destroyer and returned to his own home high in the Andes mountains.

25

The boat that was supposed to take me, Esme, and Becker ashore—or maybe López and Becker—had left late with only Becker and a crowd of excited Galapaguinos aboard. It returned, on schedule, three weeks later.

For me, and I think for Ana too, those three weeks were sheer pleasure. The murders had been solved, I'd been saved from a fate worse than death, and now I found myself living a dream life in paradise. All the same, I wished I'd managed to get to know the baroness just a little bit better. To understand her complexities, to know more about her dreams and joys and terrors. To learn just what sort of fantasy—light or dark—she was trying to create for herself. Did she build a castle with a tower to remind her of a happy childhood or to protect her from her enemies? To find the answer to the question Ana had asked the first time I met her: Do sirens sing their songs intentionally to trap sailors, or do they sing because it's their nature to sing?

And once again, I knew that I would never know these answers. Like the truth about the Crazy German, the whole truth about Baroness Ilse von Arndt would remain shrouded in the mists that so often hide these most illusive islands.

Curious to see what new surprises the ship might bring, Ana and I were standing at the land end of the pier watching the ship nose up to the dock. As it moored, the excited crowd hopped and waved. Among them I spotted Gregor and Kaspar trying to clear a space on the pier, right under one of the booms. "You think that's the new icebox they're waiting for?" I asked Ana.

"I bet it is."

"I wonder how he got it so quickly. How did he pay for it without sending money to the mainland?"

"He must have asked somebody ashore to loan it to him. That's a lesson for you, Fred. The power of love. Carla's wanted a new one for a year or two." Ana was laughing quietly; I was trying to keep up by smiling dutifully at the suggestion of domestic blackmail.

Out of the corner of my eye I saw Esme walking toward the dock. She was still limping, but she looked much better than she had. And happy to be in Wreck Bay's messy, waterlogged plaza rather than the bitter streets of Guayaquil. I smiled at her. She smiled back and nodded respectfully to Ana.

My eyes returned to the crowd on the pier and settled on the face of one of the passengers beginning to make their way in our direction. A bolt of shock, then fear, blasted through me. I recognized the face; it belonged to a guy from New York named Giorgio Rizzo—or "Georgie the Meathook" to his friends. Rizzo worked for the same people who'd employed the little thug I shot; he was one of their toughest enforcers. There was another face alongside Rizzo's. I couldn't put a name to it, but I knew it belonged to another enforcer. I felt as if I'd been kicked in the gut. They hadn't forgotten me, and I knew that even if war did break out from one corner of the world to the other they still wouldn't forget.

The Meathook's eyes scanned the crowd but didn't show any hint of recognition as they passed over me.

López, God damn him! It was as if he'd risen from his grave to get me. He must have contacted New York before Becker shot him. I tried to reassure myself that they wouldn't recognize me. Not in shorts and an undershirt, skinnier than before and wearing a full head of long, almost bushy hair now sun-bleached to a chalky, brittle gray-black. But in time I'd get a haircut—Ana was already making remarks—and in time they'd find me. The Mob didn't send fools on jobs like this. Not all the way out here.

"You look like a guy who could benefit from a leisurely sea cruise," said a voice from behind me.

Impulsively, I reached for Ana's arm. She was the only thing in the world now worth anything to me, and I'd be God damned if I'd leave her. I turned and found Thompson standing there. "You're right," he said. "She's why you'll come with us. If you stay she'll end up just as dead as you will."

My grip on Ana's arm tightened. She looked at me. She understood what Thompson meant as well as I did. She and Don Vicente had friends in New York too. She'd known all along.

"Listen, Freiman, a war's coming, one even bigger than the last one, and your country has uses for you. I'm willing to bet the lady will wait for you."

Shaking with indignation, fear, and confusion, I looked out at Thompson's schooner as it swung at anchor. Was I to be the Dutchman who was cursed to race around and around the world forever? I didn't like Thompson one bit, but I realized that he was my only chance. I felt Ana's free hand on my cheek, turning my face toward her. I felt her breath and then the pressure of her lips and the grace of her body against mine. "I'll wait for you, Fred. I'll never find another playmate like you. Never. Remember, I'm a modern woman. I make my own choices and I stick with them."